WEST OF THE BRAZOS

Texas Ranger Sam Buck has a double assignment as he heads towards Goldwell: to recapture escaped convict Dick Conroy and to assist County Sheriff Emerson to apprehend an assassin who kills and robs, then disappears without trace. When he least expects it, Sam meets the killer, only to discover he is not the only crack shot with a rifle on the prowl. Sam Buck will need more lives than the proverbial cat if he is to survive all the bullets coming his way...

WEST OF THE BRAZOS

For
Harold Porter
one of the old-time Westerners

WEST OF THE BRAZOS

by

Bret Rey

Dales Large Print Books
Long Preston, North Yorkshire,
BD23 4ND, England.

British Library Cataloguing in Publication Data.

Rey, Bret
    W est of the Brazos

    A catalogue record of this book is
    available from the British Library

    ISBN   1-84137-018-5 pbk

First published in Great Britain by Robert Hale Ltd., 1995

Published in Large Print 2000 by arrangement with Robert Hale
Ltd.

Dales Large Print is an imprint of Library Magna Books Ltd.

Printed and bound in Great Britain by
T.J. (International) Ltd., Cornwall, PL28 8RW

ONE

On a hillock to the east of the road into town, Bert Vernon rested his rifle between two small rocks he had placed in position, watching, sombre-eyed, the approach of the big grey and its rider. Let them come another half mile closer, just to make sure it really was Chuck Felton in the saddle and to bring him within easy range of the Winchester Model 1866 rifle.

The grey seemed to take a long time to cover that half mile at walking pace, but then Vernon set the rifle sight on the man's belt buckle to allow for the bullet to strike where it would be most lethal. Aim at six o'clock on your target, he had been schooled years earlier, then you have a chance of a bull's eye.

He gently squeezed the trigger until the

rifle bucked against his shoulder. The grey reared as its rider fell from the saddle.

Vernon's mouth was a tight line, unsmiling between the heavy brown moustache and untidy beard, but inwardly he felt a sense of exultancy. He got to his feet and ambled to his own mount, put his left boot into the stirrup, swung his right leg over the saddle and rode away. The killing was finished. The last of the men who had cheated him of the good life had bitten the dust. Now he could begin again, but for that he needed money. He would wait a little while before he visited the widow. She would be more receptive to the shock coming her way if he gave her a few days to accustom herself to life without her husband.

TWO

Sam Buck drew rein and dismounted, fisted his Colt pistol and walked slowly towards the man lying on the trail.

'You hurt bad, mister?'

There was no response and Buck turned the body over with his right boot. Even as he looked into grey eyes that would never look back again, Buck knew that somebody had turned the man into a corpse.

He looked around him. Some two hundred yards away a big grey gelding was grazing contentedly. Buck holstered his gun and strolled towards the horse, wondering if it might be spooked by a stranger. The gelding lifted his head and stared back with equine curiosity. It made no protest as the tall man took hold of the reins. He led the horse back to where the body lay.

'Stay there now, boy, stay there.'

Buck wondered how he was going to get the corpse up onto the grey without getting some of the congealing blood on the man's shirt on to his own clothing. He shrugged with resignation. As he lifted the corpse the grey whinnied his aversion to the smell of blood. When Buck attempted to lift the corpse across the vacant saddle the grey edged away. It took him some time to calm the horse and hump the body over.

He led the grey and its grisly burden towards his own sorrel, climbed into the saddle and headed for town. As he rode down Main Street folks stared, first at the corpse, then at him.

'It's Felton!' one man exclaimed after he had bent his head to get a look at the face of the dead man.

That's one small mystery solved, Buck mused, having decided earlier to allow the town marshal to go through the man's pockets. The stranger's pronouncement did little to resolve the questions that had prowled around Buck's think-box.

Outside the town marshal's office he halted, just as the lawman emerged, six feet two inches of him, through the doorway.

The broad shouldered marshal looked first at the corpse, then up at Buck. 'Where'd you find him?'

'About four miles back along the trail. Shot from a distance, is my guess.'

Buck slid to the ground. 'I heard somebody call him Felton. He must be known around here.'

'He is.' The marshal turned to the man who had first identified the body. 'Take him along to Herman, will ya?'

'Sure thing, Marshal.'

Invited into the office, Buck hitched his sorrel and followed the marshal inside, closing the door behind him, to the chagrin of the onlookers. Buck was past being surprised about the general public's morbid curiosity with death.

'You must be Marshal Brundle.'

'That's right? Who are you?'

'Corporal Sam Buck, Texas Rangers.'

There was no badge on Buck's vest and that fact prompted Brundle to ask for identification. Buck reached into a pocket and offered the marshal his authority. Satisfied, Brundle handed it back. 'Take a seat, Mr Buck.'

Brundle lowered himself into a wing-backed chair as Buck accepted the invitation. 'Who is this feller, Marshal?'

'Chuck Felton. He has – had – a ranch nine miles out o' town. Some o' the best grazin' there is along the Brazos.'

'Why would anyone want to kill him?'

'I don't know.'

'Any known killers in town?'

'Not unless they came in overnight. We do get gun-crazy kids every so often.'

'Whoever killed Felton was no gun-crazy kid.'

'How d'you know that?'

'He was shot from a distance by an expert rifleman. The hole in his chest was directly in front of his heart.'

'You mean it was a professional killin'?'

Buck lifted his shoulders in a gesture of indecision. 'More than likely, but there's no way of knowing at this stage. A clear case of assassination, though. Whoever fired that shot knows how to use a rifle, that's for sure.'

'I guess it's up to the county sheriff to sort this one out. Felton was killed outside my territory.'

'Four miles outside town is not very far, Marshal. I reckon the county sheriff might figure you could help him on this one.'

Brundle grinned. 'I guess he might at that. He is kinda busy right now. This is not the first unsolved killin' in the county lately. Any more an' it'll be like an epidemic.'

Buck was trying to decide how much trust he could put in the marshal. He already knew something about him, but apart from a shady past, there was nothing of late known against him. He had been elected fair and square and, as far as Buck knew, he was in nobody's pay.

'You have a reputation with a gun yourself, Marshal.'

'That's what got me elected, Corporal, only my rep is with a hand gun, not a Winchester.'

Buck smiled disarmingly. 'So I heard.'

'What else did you hear about me?'

The marshal had removed his hat to reveal a sparse head of gingery-brown hair and a forehead already deeply lined. Buck remembered that Brundle was forty-three years old, had been married and then widowed by an outlaw's bullet, but had remained law-abiding ever since he had caught up with his wife's killer.

'You were a bit of a tearaway in your younger days. You were sentenced to serve three years in the Penitentiary for robbery when you were nineteen; reputed to have killed eleven men in what were called fair fights.'

'They were.'

'I'll take your word for it.' Buck deliberately omitted to mention Brundle's marriage and the manner in which he had lost his wife. 'You've been town marshal here for nigh on five years.'

'Expect to get elected next time around, too.'

'You've earned the reputation of being a good lawman.'

Brundle did not smile as he put the question, 'That puts me in your good books, does it?'

Buck smiled easily. 'I'm gonna trust you, Marshal. Sheriff Emerson has asked for help with these killings. Now I'm asking for yours. Looks to me as if this Chuck Felton is one more in the chain. If we can find out why he was killed, maybe that will lead us to the killer, or whoever has instigated the killings.'

'I've talked it over with Sheriff Emerson, but it baffles us both. We know of no connection between the dead men.'

'They have all been rifle shot,' Buck said, 'so the indications are that they were all killed by the same man.' Then he added,

'Or woman.'

'Woman!' Brundle stared back at him, shocked by such an amazing possibility.

Buck smiled back at him. 'Don't look so startled, Marshal. Fact is I've met more than one woman who could shoot better than most men with a long gun.'

'The hell you say! Well I can tell you one thing, Corporal Buck, there's no such woman livin' around here.'

'I don't figure our killer comes from around here. Maybe nowhere west of the Brazos; maybe not even Texas.'

Brundle chewed over what Buck was implying, then said, 'That might be a startin' point, Corporal. If we could find out where all these dead men came from, maybe we'd see the connection.'

'Just what I've been thinking.'

Brundle leaned forward, his arms resting on his desk. 'Felton came from Philadelphia, and so did Kerrigan.'

'Kerrigan?'

'Lived in Austin but travelled a lot. The

two men knew each other. Kerrigan was believed to be headin' back home after visitin' Chuck Felton. I wonder how long they'd known each other?'

'Could be hard to find out now they're both dead.'

'Not so, Corporal. Let's you an' me take a ride out to the Felton ranch. His wife should be able to tell us. Somebody has to break the bad news to her, an' I guess that's one job I can save Sheriff Emerson.'

'Hadn't you best check Felton's pockets first?'

'Might be a good idea, but before we go down to Herman's place, don't...'

Buck interrupted. 'Herman?'

'Herman Reeves. The mortician.'

Buck stored the name in his memory.

'As I was about to suggest, Mr Buck, it might be prudent for you to change that blood-stained shirt afore we visit Mrs Felton. You can use the back room.'

Herman Reeves had stripped the body and

was washing it down when the two law officers arrived at his place.

'Been through his pockets, Herman?' Brundle queried.

'Not yet, Marshal.' He nodded towards a pile of clothing draped over a bench seat. 'Help yourself.'

The bloodied shirt had two pockets and the marshal picked it up gingerly. 'I'll hold it, Mr Buck, while you see what he was carryin'.'

There was a small folded notecase containing one hundred and twenty dollars in one pocket, a stub of pencil and three scraps of paper in the other. Brundle dropped the shirt back on the seat and the two men unfolded and read the notes. One was an IOU for five hundred dollars, with a signature that was not hard to decipher.

'Who is Elaine Tarrant?' Buck inquired.

'Runs the hotel down the street. She's havin' an extension built, an' maybe she didn't want to go to the bank for a loan.'

Buck turned his head sideways to fix his

eyes on the marshal. 'She was friendly with Felton?'

'I guess you could say that. She fed him when he was in town. Elaine was also friendly with Irma Felton, so don't read more into it than you should.'

'I don't reckon she'd kill him for five hundred bucks.'

'I don't think she knows one end of a rifle from the other,' the marshal returned, 'an' she'd hardly find it worthwhile to hire a killer for that five hundred.'

Herman Reeves was drying his hands as he moved towards them. He watched as the two lawmen went through Felton's pants pockets. They produced some loose coinage, a handkerchief, a folding pocket knife, but nothing to give even a hint that would help them.

'Ain't you gonna introduce me, Marshal?' Reeves asked.

The two men glanced at each other, Brundle waiting for Buck to take the initiative.

'Can you keep your mouth shut, Mr Reeves?'

Affronted, Reeves replied, 'I guess I'll leave the marshal to answer that question for me.'

'This is Corporal Sam Buck, Herman. He's from the Texas Rangers, but right now we're keepin' that to ourselves.'

Reeves looked back at the dark-haired, handsome Ranger. 'I'll respect your confidence, Corporal.'

'Call me Sam. Sounds better in the hearing of other folks.'

'Glad to know you, Sam. I hope you catch this killer.'

'You know anyone who might want Felton dead?'

'Several. Not everybody loved him.'

THREE

The eyes of the short, lean mortician rested steadily on Buck, challenging him to pursue the matter.

Buck responded bluntly. 'You care to name names, Mr Reeves?'

'I bury men, Mr Buck. I'm in no hurry to become a candidate for my own funeral parlour.' He laughed. 'Who'd take on the responsibility for my buryin'?'

Buck's response was like a bullet striking granite. 'If you can throw any light on this killing it's your civic duty to do it.'

'No hard evidence, Mr Buck, only suspicions. A man with all the money Chuck Felton must've had soon finds enmity.'

'Richer than most ranchers, huh?'

'Let me put it this way. He came to Goldwell with enough of the stuff to pay cash money for a spread that must be the best west o' the Brazos. What folks have asked is how did he make it? On the backs of the men who were slaughtered in the war between north and south?'

Buck knew Reeves was suggesting the dead man had made his pile in the munitions manufacturing industry. He said quietly, 'Men getting killed always makes money for somebody, Mr Reeves. Even you.'

'And how about you, Mr Buck? Ain't you in the killin' business?'

'Only when it becomes unavoidable.'

'Like hunting down a man so's you can hang 'im?'

'The Good Book says a man who takes a life must forfeit his own,' the Ranger reminded the mortician.

'I guess you'd know more about that than me.'

'Maybe.'

Marshal Brundle chipped in, 'We'll leave you now, Herman. Have to ride out an' tell

Irma she's a widow an' hand over this money an' things.'

'I don't envy you that job, but while you're there, tell her I'd appreciate instructions about what to do with the body. She might have some special wishes about the funeral.'

'I'll do that, Herman. Be seein' you.'

They rode side by side out of town, heading north along the trail Buck had come in on.

'You think that Reeves knows something, Marshal?'

'He might, but he is known for his sense of wry humour.'

'You mean he likes stirring things up?'

'That's one way of puttin' it, Sam.'

They took an hour to reach the ranch house, exchanging a few confidences on the way, by which time the Ranger had a fair idea of the truth about what had been previously said about the richness of the grazing land. Even in early June the Texas sun had not sucked all the green out of the pasture.

Irma Felton had turned forty, in Buck's estimation. Wide, dark eyes looked him over from beneath arched brows. Under short chestnut hair her forehead was faintly lined. She offered Buck her hand in welcome after Brundle had introduced them, giving the Texas Ranger his full title.

'I'm sorry we couldn't meet under different circumstances, Mrs Felton.'

She frowned. 'That remark suggests you've come with bad news, Mr Buck. How does it concern me?'

Buck glanced at Brundle, who nodded almost imperceptibly. Buck said, 'Your husband, Mrs Felton.' He paused to allow her to steel herself against the shock of the coming news. 'I found him on the trail this morning. He's dead. I'm sorry.'

Her eyes glazed as the news penetrated her brain. 'Dead? How? Not one of those awful heart attacks, surely? He was as strong as a bull.'

'He was shot, Mrs Felton. Murdered.'

She swayed on her feet and Brundle

hurried forward to steady her. 'Come an' sit down, ma'am.'

He guided her to a plush leather armchair. She lowered herself into its embrace. 'Can I get you something?' Brundle asked.

'No.' She passed a hand across her brow. 'I'll be all right in a moment.' She looked up at the two men, unwilling to believe what she had been told. 'Are you sure it's Chuck?'

'There's no mistake, ma'am,' Brundle answered, the lines on his forehead deepening. 'I'm truly sorry.'

Buck said, 'Have you any brandy in the house, Mrs Felton? It might fortify you.'

'Yes.' She was badly shaken. 'Yes, yes, it might. In that cupboard behind you, if you would be so kind.'

Buck poured her a good measure, then bent to hand it to her. She looked into his brown eyes. 'Why, Mr Buck? Who? Who would want to kill my husband?'

'We were hoping you might be able to throw some light on that yourself, ma'am. You might know if he had any enemies?'

She took a sip of the brandy, but her face was a mask of confusion. They couldn't even guess what she was thinking.

'It's been suggested he might have made enemies,' Buck said after a long silence. 'Do you know of any?'

'Who told you that?'

Buck's shoulders lifted as he smiled. 'Rumours will fly around in towns like Goldwell, ma'am.'

'You mean...'

It was a line he did not wish to follow and so he cut in, 'Tell me about your life back east, Mrs Felton. There might be a clue there somewhere.'

Her eyes lowered and the fingers of one hand entwined with the other. Buck sensed that she was debating with herself how much to tell the two men. She glanced from one to the other, as if wondering if she could trust them to keep some secret that was locked away in her mind.

Buck prompted her. 'What made your husband decide to bring you out West?'

'He felt there was so much crime and corruption in Philadelphia and he didn't want our three daughters to become tainted with it. He said we could have a good life here in Texas.'

Marshal Brundle handed her the money and the IOU he had taken from her husband's pockets, then stood aside, too uncomfortable to take any part in the questioning of this woman he looked upon as a friend. Buck turned away and strolled to the window, then swivelled on his heels and faced the woman again.

'Pardon me for asking, ma'am, but how did your husband react to the death of Jack Kerrigan? They were business partners back in Philadelphia, I believe.'

'Yes, they were. Chuck was upset by Jack's murder.'

'Were they involved in any of this corruption you mentioned? I ask because they were both killed by the same method.'

To his relief she was not offended by the question. 'I'm not sure, Mr Buck, but I think they might have been too close to it for comfort.'

Could it be mere coincidence that the two men had moved to Texas about the same time? Buck asked himself.

'You think they could have made enemies back East?'

'Chuck never admitted it, and I never asked.'

'But you think it's possible?'

She hesitated only for a moment. 'He seemed tense the last few months we were there. Without telling me, he'd been negotiating to buy this ranch long before we moved. He's been so much more relaxed since we've been here, as if a great weight had been lifted from his shoulders.'

'And your daughters... How have they taken to ranch life?'

'Very well, actually. Of course we've been here for three years now and they've all matured in that time.' Her face clouded. 'How ever am I going to tell them their father has been murdered?'

The question was directed at herself and not at the two men. Buck wondered when she was going to crack and break into tears. She seemed to be holding up well for a woman unaccustomed to the raw life of Texas and being suddenly deprived of her protector.

'Where are your daughters now, Mrs Felton?'

She fixed her eyes on him again. 'Out riding. All of them have taken to horses very well. I'm afraid I haven't. Animals scare me.'

Brundle turned to look out of the window, his attention caught by sound the woman had not heard. 'They're riding in now, ma'am. Best decide what you're gonna tell them.'

Buck said, 'They'll want to know why, ma'am, and right now me and the marshal don't have any answers.'

FOUR

As the two lawmen rode back to Goldwell, each with his own thoughts, Buck's imminent need was to find the county sheriff. Marshal Brundle was not privy to the sheriff's movements and Buck's pre-arranged meeting with Sheriff Emerson in Goldwell was not until tomorrow. Emerson would not yet know about the killing of Chuck Felton, but once he did, would it offer some clue to the reason for all the earlier killings, particularly in view of the fact that Jack Kerrigan had been a friend of Felton's?

It seemed reasonable to assume that Emerson had already explored all possible avenues of information in Goldwell, but this most recent killing might open up new lines of inquiry locally. According to Marshal

Brundle, little was known in Goldwell about Chuck Felton's past. The man had apparently played his cards very close to his chest, yet most men make a slip of the tongue now and then and someone might know something of importance, without even realising the value of the information. Buck decided he would explore the saloons and talk with the locals.

'What's your next move, Sam?' Brundle queried as they both dismounted outside the marshal's office.

'Think I'll book me a bed at the hotel first, then I'll make the acquaintance of some of the townsfolk.'

'If you don't want folks to know you're a Ranger, what's your cover story?'

'I'm just passing through on my way to Houston. It'll be all over town by now that I'm the one who brought in Chuck Felton, so I reckon nobody'll query me taking an interest.'

'Not after you rode out with me to the Felton ranch, they won't. The whole town'll know about that by now for sure.'

'I'm due to meet with Sheriff Emerson tomorrow, but if he should get back to town tonight, you might tell him I'm here.'

'I'll do that. I'll tell him about you findin' Felton an' then ridin' out with me to tell the widow while I'm at it.'

'Thanks, Marshal.'

In the Shady Lady Saloon a few minutes before six o'clock Ranger Sam Buck ran smack into Leonard Otis, a twenty-year-old killer who had eluded capture five months earlier after the killing of a town marshal in West Texas. Otis recognised Sam Buck immediately and his hands flew to his twin-holstered ivory-handled Colts before a word could be exchanged. He was not as fast on the draw as he had kidded himself and Sam shot him through the heart as Otis hauled his weapons from leather. They clattered to the saloon floor just before his body tippled backwards in a death fall.

Buck glanced around him to see if any

other gunnie was in the saloon, looking for trouble, before he walked towards the prone figure, gun still in his hand. As he holstered it he looked at the barkeep and said, 'I guess somebody ought to go get the marshal.'

'I'm right behind you, Sam,' Brundle called from the door. 'I was just passin'' when I heard the shot. What happened?'

'He drew on me as soon as we saw each other. Leonard Otis. He was wanted for killing a marshal a while back.'

'You think he could be the one who killed Felton?'

'No, I don't. If you check his horse I doubt if you'll find a long gun in the saddle boot.'

The deep-chested marshal, a commanding presence, looked around him. 'Anybody know what this feller was doin' here?'

'He was just havin' a drink, Marshal,' the barkeep volunteered.

'You wouldn't happen to know his horse, would you?'

'No, I wouldn't, but I reckon there ain't too many strange mounts hitched outside.'

'I'll take a look. One o' you fellers go get Herman. Tell 'im to bring a pine box.'

As Brundle went outside, Buck ambled towards the bar. 'I could use a cold beer, mister.'

'I guess you two knew each other, huh?' the man said as he pushed a glass towards the Ranger.

'Not hard to work that out, considering he went for his guns as soon as he saw me,' Buck answered non-committally. Allowing the barkeep to think he'd had a personal feud with Leonard Otis seemed like a good idea.

The marshal came back into the saloon and strode purposefully towards Buck. 'I seem to recall gettin' a Wanted poster about this hombre, Sam, but then I get a lot of 'em. It was some time back an' I guess I'd forgotten. There's a buckskin hitched out there, an' you were right – no long gun.'

'Try checking with the Ranger Office in Austin, Marshal. I'm sure they'll confirm what I've told you.'

'I guess this puts you in line for the reward money, Sam,' Brundle said loud enough for everyone in the saloon to hear.

Buck played up to him, smiling broadly. 'Yes, I guess it does. I can always use an extra dollar.'

'An extra thousand dollars, you mean.'

There were only four other men present and they all strolled towards the bar. The conversation soon got around to the fact that it was Sam Buck who had found Chuck Felton's body on the trail that morning, making it easy for Buck to ask a few questions, but none of the answers gave an inkling to who the killer might be.

Herman Reeves arrived with a pine box and was given assistance to take the body away.

'Will you be in town for long, Mr Buck?' one of the men asked.

'I'm on my way to Houston, but there's no hurry. I'm curious to find out who killed Chuck Felton.'

'You and everybody in Goldwell. It just

don't make sense.'

'It does to the killer,' the marshal said.

It was after dark when the county sheriff arrived in town. He stabled his black mare and then looked in on the town marshal. Brundle told him what had happened during the day and where he could find Ranger Sam Buck.

'I don't know his reasons, Sheriff, but he asked me and Herman Reeves to keep quiet about his status and reason for bein' here, so I guess he intends to play a casual hand. Mebbe he figures he'll be more useful t'you if he doesn't reveal you sent for help.'

'He could be right. I'll look in on him when I book in to the hotel. Shouldn't be hard to find his room number.'

'I suppose you're no nearer to findin' out who killed Kerrigan?'

'No, but I think I know why and who *might* have done it.'

'Anybody we know?'

'No. A man from Philadelphia, if my

information is correct.'

'We figured it might have had somethin' t'do with his past,' Brundle reminded him. 'You got a name for this hombre?'

'I have, but if you don't mind I'll keep it to myself for the time being. I'm still waiting for more information before I can be certain he's the right man.'

Brundle shrugged. 'None o' my concern, less'n he shows up here in town.'

'He might well do that, but I doubt it.'

'If you're right, he's probably headed back to Philadelphia by now.'

The sheriff got to his feet, let out a sigh of weariness, then said, 'I hope not. It's a long ride to Philadelphia.' He summoned a wry smile. 'Besides, it's outside my bailiwick.'

'So whoever he is, he could still get away with it.'

FIVE

Sam Buck opened the door to find a man with a thick head of light brown hair and piercing brown eyes gazing at him.

'Sam Buck?'

The Ranger didn't need telling that this was Sheriff Emerson. The full-lipped mouth was partially hidden by a thick moustache. A strong face with a dimpled chin, just as Marshal Brundle had described him. 'Come on in.'

He stood aside and then closed the door as the man said, 'I'm the county sheriff. It was me who sent for you.'

'Take the chair, Sheriff. I'll sit on the bed.'

Emerson lowered his huge, amply covered frame. Buck noticed a thickening of the waistline, but the sheriff was not yet running to fat. A man who probably packed a hard, heavy punch if the need should arise. Sam was glad they were on the same side.

'Marshal Brundle tells me you've already been active here in town, as well as coming across Chuck Felton's body.'

Buck nodded, but said nothing.

The sheriff went on, 'You think the widow was completely frank with you about not knowing Chuck Felton had enemies?'

'I got that impression. She couldn't understand why anyone would want to kill him, but she did hint there'd been some kind of improper practice back in Philadelphia.'

'She was right. Shady dealings in the business world back there. I wired a friend in Philadelphia and he's doing some investigations right now. It could be a few days, or even a week before I get more information.'

Emerson went on to reveal that both Chuck Felton and Jack Kerrigan had been associated with a man by the name of Neville Pardoe, a smart eastern lawyer who knew all the legal ways to fleece the unsuspecting of their hard-won assets.

'I find it significant, Mr Buck, that Pardoe, Kerrigan, and now Felton are all dead.'

'All shot?'

'Yes, but with one unmatched difference. Pardoe was shot with a Smith and Wesson handgun. Kerrigan was gunned down by a sniper with a rifle and, according to the marshal, so was Felton.'

'Doesn't mean they weren't all killed by the same man, Sheriff. If your friend in Philadelphia can find anyone with sufficient motive, at least in his own eyes, then that's the one we should be looking for.'

'Bertram Vernon. Former U.S. Cavalryman and an expert rifle shot. He started a small freight business, carrying passengers and goods between Philadelphia and the cities and towns within a hundred mile radius. Needed money to expand and borrowed from Kerrigan and Felton. Went bust when they foreclosed before he had time to get himself out of the red.'

'Enough to turn some men into killers, I suppose.'

'That's my feeling. I've asked my old friend in Philli to find out what happened to Vernon. We don't even know where to start looking.'

'If he's the one, he was in Texas this morning.'

'And on the way out now, is my guess.'

Buck knew the prognosis was more than likely, but if this Vernon had accomplished what he had set out to do, what then? He put the question to Emerson. 'If you've got the right suspect, Sheriff, and this Vernon has taken revenge, what will he do now? He has to start over but, without money, his options are limited.'

'He might rejoin the cavalry, or he could go to work for some other freight company.'

'Too early to check with the Army people. I guess we'll have to be patient for a while.'

'I'll ride out to see Irma Felton in the morning. Brundle tells me she's having Chuck buried on the ranch. Maybe she knows something about this Bert Vernon.'

Buck nodded and considered his position,

then said, 'I've a lot on my plate right now, Sheriff, so I guess I'll leave you to it for a week or so. I can't afford to be kicking my heels around Goldwell while you wait for answers from Philadelphia.'

Emerson understood and raised no objections. 'Meet me back here in ten days, Mr Buck. Can you do that? Just in case I'm on the wrong track.'

'I'll do my best, Sheriff.' There was something that puzzled Buck. 'What I don't understand is why you sent to the Ranger Office for help with this Kerrigan killing.'

'It wasn't just that, Mr Buck. I've had four mysterious killings besides Kerrigan to figure out. I was maybe a mite hasty in sending for you, but at the time I thought all five were connected.'

'And now you don't?'

'If I'm right about this Vernon feller, no, I don't. But I'm still stumped over the other four.'

'I reckon you'd best tell me about them.'

Sam Buck recalled Marshal Brundle

saying that any more killings in the county would amount to an epidemic. Emerson told him what he knew about the men who had been killed. Seemingly there had been no known connection between the four of them. None had any obvious links with Jack Kerrigan or Chuck Felton.

Boris Dillinger had been the blacksmith in Goldwell but he'd gotten itchy feet and sold out. Two days later he was found dead on the Austin trail, head-shot, his brains splattered, his pockets fleeced of money.

Ignatius Jordon had been clubbed to death on the banks of the Brazos River. Jordon was a drifter, unable to settle to any one thing for long, always looking for new pastures, scratching a living where and when he could, doing odd jobs for anyone who would employ him. Seldom had more than a few dollars to rattle in his pockets.

'As far as Dillinger was concerned it seemed like a plain case of robbery,' the sheriff said, 'but that hardly applies in the case of Jordon. He was an inoffensive little man who wouldn't hurt a fly or pick a quarrel with anyone. Then there was Harold Lashley.'

Lashley was a third rate gunnie who knew his limitations, according to the sheriff. The town marshal had locked him up a time or two when he had gotten the worse for drink, more for his own safety than anything else. Under the influence of too much drink he forgot those limitations and Marshal Brundle, who despised the man, did not want Lashley to become the victim of some galoot taking an unfair advantage. Brundle did what he could to avoid killings on the streets and in the saloons of Goldwell.

'And who was the fourth man?' Buck asked.

'Alf Morrison. He owned the Beer House here in town.'

'Then finding his killer was surely Brundle's job, not yours.'

'Not so, Mr Buck. Alf was taking a trip to Austin at the time, too, and like Dillinger and Kerrigan, he was rifle shot.'

Three men killed by an expert rifle shot, Buck mused, and now Chuck Felton. He could understand how Emerson had figured there was some connection between all the killings, until he had learned something of Felton's association with Jack Kerrigan back in Philadelphia. The fact that Ignatius Jordon had been clubbed to death rather than shot did not prove there was no link to all the deaths. The drifter's demise looked like an isolated incident, but if his death was related to the others it might be that he had discovered who murdered Jack Kerrigan and Boris Dillinger and had then gotten too close to the killer.

Buck said, 'One man could have killed them all, Sheriff, but the odds against seem a mite long. Chuck Felton was not robbed.'

'I see that now. Maybe when you get back from Houston we could work together on them all?'

'This man who owned the Beer House here in town...'

'Alf Morrison.'

'Yes, Morrison. Was there any bad blood between him and any of the other saloon owners?'

'I doubt it. Morrison was small fry by comparison. As far as I know he had nobody gunning for him. He was content just to make a living. Not one of your ambitious men, out to make a fortune and retire to the coast, but robbed, just like the others.'

Buck shrugged his shoulders. 'Well, it's getting late, Sheriff. I'll see if I can find out anything about any of these men while I'm in Houston. We can talk when I get back.'

'We'll do that, Mr Buck. Whatever your business in Houston, I wish you luck.'

'I may need it. I'm on the trail of a young killer who tricked his escort and escaped while on his way to jail in Waco. We heard he'd been seen in Houston.'

Emerson's lips moved in a suggestion of a smile. 'They do say the best place for a man to hide is in the big city.'

It rained during the night, but by the time

Sam Buck had saddled his sorrel the sun was already sucking the damp from the street. He headed south for Houston.

Well accustomed to the heat of Texas, he nevertheless sought shelter as noontime approached. There was a small town no more than three miles ahead and he decided to seek a meal there and find shade for his sorrel.

It was a small establishment and filled with customers as he pushed his way through the door. There was only one seat vacant, at a table for two, and the girl sitting there was strikingly pretty. He moved towards her and said, 'Do you mind if I join you? It seems a mite crowded right now.'

She looked into his brown eyes, noted the strong, handsome face and felt something move inside her. She wanted to offer him a welcoming smile but the thumping in her chest made her nervous. For years she had tolerated the lustful stares of men but she had never been attracted so strongly to one until now.

'You're welcome,' she said between perfectly shaped lips.

Buck settled himself and favoured her with a smile that had melted many a female resistance in the past. 'You live here?' he asked her.

'No. I'm on my way to see my uncle in Goldwell.'

'Now there's a coincidence. I came from there this morning. How are you travelling?'

'I have a pony outside.'

'You're riding alone?'

'Yes.'

He tried not to show his astonishment that such a pretty young woman would risk being accosted by some of the riff-raff that rode the trails. 'Where have you come from?'

'Wilton. I helped my mother to run an eating house there, but she died last week and I didn't want to stay there after that.'

'This uncle of yours ... He's expecting you?'

The waitress came to ask for his order

before the girl had a chance to reply. Buck asked for whatever was available. 'I'm not fussy at this time of the day.'

When the waitress departed the Ranger looked questioningly at the girl again. 'Oh, I should introduce myself. I'm Sam Buck.'

'Glad to know you, Mr Buck. I'm Melissa Nevin. My uncle is the blacksmith in Goldwell, but he doesn't know I'm coming. He is my mother's younger brother.'

Buck's face clouded and the girl noticed his change of expression. 'Do I get the feeling you don't like my uncle?'

'I never met him, Miss Nevin, but I'm afraid I have bad news for you. Your uncle was murdered two weeks ago.'

'Murdered! I don't believe it!'

SIX

He allowed time for her astonishment to resolve itself into acceptance, anticipating the dismay that would surely follow.

Once she realised that he was not being inconsiderate she said, 'How? Who did it?'

'He was shot. I don't know who did it.'

'Isn't anybody doing anything about it?'

'County Sheriff Emerson thinks robbery was the motive, but so far he has no suspects. A lot of people knew your uncle had sold his business and was on his way to Austin when he was killed.'

Now came the dismay. 'Sold his business! Oh, no! What am I going to do?'

'You have no other relatives you could go to?'

'No.'

The waitress arrived with steak, potatoes,

biscuits and thick gravy and he looked at the plate with relish before fashioning a smile that made her blush. 'Thanks.'

He picked up his knife and fork and began to eat.

'If there is anything I can do, Miss Nevin...?'

'My mother always told me that if anything ever happened to her I should go and stay with Uncle Boris. It's four years since we've seen him, but we thought he had settled down in Goldwell. He was a bit of a drifter when he was younger, but once he'd set himself up in Goldwell we thought he was content.'

Buck masticated what was in his mouth before commenting, 'A man can get bored with the same old routine day after day, Miss Nevin.'

'Is that why he sold up and left?'

'That's what I've been told.'

'You don't live in Goldwell?'

He smiled again. 'How did you guess?'

'You said you'd never met my uncle.'

She was sharp all right, Buck decided. 'No, but I'll be going back there in a few days from now. I promised Sheriff Emerson I'd give him what help I could.'

'Why would you want to do that?'

It would have been easy to tell her the whole truth, but then she might let it slip in Goldwell that he was a Texas Ranger and for the time being he preferred to keep that between himself and the three men who already knew and had agreed not to blow his cover.

'He's got a big investigation on right now, so he asked if I would give him a hand.'

'Are you some kind of detective?'

He laughed softly. 'I've never been accused of that.'

She persisted. 'Then why would the county sheriff ask for your help? What do you know that makes him think...?'

'Every citizen should help the law whenever they can, Miss,' he interrupted, hoping to put her head at ease.

He could almost read the doubts chasing

through her head.

'I suppose so,' she said after he returned his attention to the food on his plate.

'What will you do now?' he asked, without looking up.

'I don't know,' she said through a long sigh. 'I have very little money, so I suppose I'll have to get a job again.'

'The eating house didn't belong to your mother?'

'No. We ran it for one of the businessmen in Wilton.'

'You wouldn't consider going back there to see if you could get your old job back?'

She hesitated for only a moment. 'No. It wouldn't be the same without Mom. Besides, I'd like to find out who killed my uncle.' She stared into space for a long moment. 'I remember he once promised he would leave me his fortune when he died. He said it like it was a joke, but if he was robbed, then his money rightfully belongs to me. Right now it would come in handy.'

'Did you know him well?'

'Not really, but I know he liked me. He used to tell me I was as pretty as a picture, but I only saw him for a few days at a time and not very often since I grew up.'

Boris Dillinger had obviously appreciated beauty, Buck mused. His description of his niece was spot on.

Buck cleared his plate, rested his elbows on the table and interlaced his fingers as he looked into her lovely brown eyes. He was concerned about her making the rest of the journey to Goldwell alone, yet he knew his duties were more important than her welfare. He battled with his conscience as he recognised that here was a maiden in distress who had taken two hard knocks, one on top of the other, and he couldn't ignore her plight.

'Forgive me for saying this, Miss Nevin, but I think you've been a mite reckless setting out alone to ride from Wilton to Goldwell. You're a very attractive young lady and there are some rough characters riding the trails these days.'

'I didn't meet any. No man accosted me.'

'Then consider yourself very fortunate, but don't push it.'

'I don't seem to have much choice, Mr Buck.'

'Please! Call me Sam, and don't take offence at what I'm going to suggest.'

'What do you mean?'

'I have to go to Houston on business and I have friends there who would put you up for a few days until I could escort you back to Goldwell myself, if you still intend to go there, that is?'

'Yes, I do. I don't see I have much option. I'd like the sheriff to know I exist, at least.'

'Then will you ride with me to Houston and wait there until I come back this way?'

She looked at him searchingly for a long time before she said, 'Why should you do this for me?'

'Because I know what can happen to girls on their own.'

'I'm hardly a girl any more, Mr ... Sam. I'm twenty-three.'

He laughed softly. 'You sure don't look it, Miss Nevin. I'd have put you at no more than eighteen.'

She said soberly, 'You're handy with the compliments, Sam. How do I know I can trust you?'

'You don't, but I've never molested any woman without an invitation.'

She smiled at that, thinking that if any man was going to molest her then she would prefer it to be Sam Buck, but she decided not to give in without at least a show of intelligent cogitation.

Into the long silence Buck said, 'You'd be safer with me than you would alone on that trail.'

A slow smile spread over her face and her eyes lit up with something he judged as relief. 'All right, Sam, I'll go with you.'

'You've made a wise decision.'

Suddenly she shot at him, 'Are you married, Sam Buck?'

'No, Melissa Nevin, I'm not, but then I could be lying about that, couldn't I?'

Their eyes held and both of them smiled. She said, 'You could, but I don't think you are. You've got an honest face.'

It quickly became apparent to Sam Buck that Melissa Nevin was no horsewoman. She had chosen sensible pants and boots and a broad-brimmed hat for her journey, but the awkward manner in which she mounted her grey pony told him her riding experience was strictly limited. A feeling of dismay shafted through him. In spite of his concern for her safety he could not help thinking he had made a mistake in taking her under his wing.

'Your pony has a lot of years behind him, I'm thinking,' he said.

'She's fourteen. Mr Ilford knew I hadn't any riding experience so he chose Bessy for me. He said she was very docile and a baby could ride her quite safely.'

They moved off at a walk and Buck remained silent until they had reached the outskirts of the small town.

'It's a long ride to Houston, Melissa. I reckon we should put the horses into a lope.'

'A lope!' Her voice was full of apprehension.

His worst fears were confirmed. 'You mean you've never ridden Bessy at more than walking pace?'

She sensed his disappointment and her reply was apologetic. 'No, never.'

He stifled a sigh of dejection, electing to instil confidence in her rather than reveal his concern. 'It's no problem, Melissa. Just shake her up a little and she'll trot, then you shake her some more and she'll lope. Try it.'

Alarm flooded her face. 'Like this,' he encouraged, and kicked his sorrel gently. The horse responded immediately, but Melissa Nevin hesitated.

He drew rein and looked back at her, summoning a smile. 'You see what I mean? Go on, try it.'

She did not want him to think her chicken-hearted, so in spite of her fears she did as he suggested. The pony began to trot and she hung on grimly, her eyes terror-stricken.

'Relax, Melissa. You'll scare your mount if she thinks you're afraid.'

When she did not immediately fall out of the saddle it seemed to come as a surprise to her and she began to sit with less rigidity. Gradually she found that she could allow her body to move with the rhythm of the pony.

Sam Buck smiled with relief. 'You see what I mean?'

'Yes. It's quite exhilarating actually.'

Best let her grow in confidence before encouraging her to ride faster. With any luck his first fears would be dispelled by the end of the day.

As they rode south he knew her mind would be full of questions about him and he decided he had to take a chance and trust her to keep quiet. They could not ride all the way to Houston in silence and he wanted her to feel complete confidence in him.

'There's something I'm going to tell you, Melissa, but I want your promise that you'll keep it to yourself for the time being.'

'I'm not a blabbermouth, Sam.'

'If I thought you were I'd never tell you.'

'Go on then, tell me.'

'The reason Sheriff Emerson asked for my help is because I'm a Texas Ranger.'

'I see. Well, now, I wonder how much more I can take in one day. You tell me my uncle has been murdered and now I find I'm riding to Houston with a Texas Ranger. I've never met one of your exclusive band before.'

His smile was broad. 'And you've learned to ride Bessy at a trot. Are you ready for the lope?'

Once again her fear reasserted itself, but she decided she must not let this man think she was a hindrance to him. 'All right. You lead off and I'll follow.'

She kicked Bessy gently and the pony responded, more because of the desire for equine company than Melissa Nevin's commands. The pony followed in the wake of the sorrel and Sam Buck's glance over his shoulder confirmed that the young woman would not be too difficult to teach. Her face was set with stern determination but she was still rising and falling rhythmically and seemed in no danger of spilling from the saddle.

After a couple of miles he decided to give the girl a break and slowed his sorrel to a walk again.

'You're doing fine, Melissa,' he told her.

'I was scared stiff, Sam.'

'Don't worry. You'll soon get to enjoy riding.'

She smiled and her eyes lit up, he was glad to note. He couldn't help wondering why such a pretty girl was unmarried.

'Are you really twenty-three, Melissa?'

'Of course. Why should I lie about my age?'

'And you've never been married?'

'No, I haven't. Why does that seem so

strange to you?'

'Hell, girl, you're the prettiest thing I've seen in ages!'

'Sam Buck! You're flirting with me!'

'No, I'm not, Melissa. I was just stating a fact. Most men would give their eye teeth to get their arms around you.' He held up his right hand to stall any protest. 'No offence intended.'

'And none taken. I've always known I was pretty, Sam, and Momma warned me about men.' The slim girl faced him squarely, concerned by what he might think of her. 'I've never been attached to any of them.'

'You don't like men?'

Her smile faded. 'My father left Momma before I was born. It was enough to make me realise I didn't want the kind of struggle to raise a child that Momma had with me.'

'I'm sorry, Melissa.'

'Don't be. I've been quite happy helping in the eating house these last few years. But now I've lost both Momma and Uncle Boris I just don't know what I'm going to do.'

He was about to make some encouraging comment when his tongue was stilled by the sound of a rifle shot.

'Wait here, Melissa! I'll come back for you!'

He sent the sorrel into a fast gallop round the bend in the trail, in search of the rifleman.

SEVEN

His eyes swept the terrain. Then he steered the sorrel under the shelter of a big oak as he spotted a man nearly a half mile away heading down the slope diagonally towards him. Buck halted and waited, watching as the rider headed for his quarry, unaware that he was under observation. Too engrossed in his grisly task to have heard the hoofbeats of my horse, Buck assumed. Away to his right a bay horse had begun to graze, the property of the victim.

The man soon reached his objective, and only moments before he threw himself out of the saddle and bent over did Sam Buck see the still form lying on the ground, half hidden by vegetation. Buck moved out of the shade, drew his rifle from the boot, and rode towards the sniper, who was busy going through his victim's pockets.

What is he looking for? Buck wondered. Money? A piece of legal paper that would be beneficial to someone else? As Buck drew closer the man dragged a moneybelt from beneath the dead man's shirt, the tails pulled out above the waistline. As he turned to remount his horse he saw Sam Buck approaching. He grabbed for his own rifle to protect himself from this unexpected interloper. Sam Buck sent a shot over his head and called out.

'Stand still or I'll put the next shot through your skull!'

Dejectedly the man's shoulders slumped and he stood waiting for Buck to join him. He must be one helluva shot, Buck mused, to be able to kill a man on horseback from the spot he had selected for his dastardly deed.

'Make a habit of this, do you?' Buck asked conversationally.

He dismounted. 'Toss that moneybelt this way, mister.'

The man silently obeyed. Buck looked him over with a practised eye. An ugly man, with ears standing out like jug handles. He stood no more than five feet eight inches, pot-bellied, and bulldog jowled, evidence of gross over-eating. He was probably younger than the thirty odd years he looked.

'Unbuckle your gunbelt.'

Round blue eyes stared back at Buck malevolently, but the rifle pointing at his midriff at a distance of no more than six feet was mighty persuasive. Slowly he unfastened the belt and let the holstered gun clump to the grass.

'Now your pants belt.'

'Pants belt! How the...?'

Buck read the thoughts passing through the ugly man's mind. 'You catch on quick,' he said.

The pants belt was tossed aside as the man grabbed at the top of his pants.

'Now lie down.'

Seething with fury but mindful of the fact that he as much as any man knew the damage a rifle bullet could do, obeyed. Sam Buck picked up the man's belt. 'Hands behind your back.'

Buck planted one foot between the man's shoulder blades, laid down his rifle and secured the man's forearms together with his own leather, pulling the buckle very tight, so much so that the killer cried out in pain.

'You can stand up now.'

After he had scrambled to his feet with some difficulty, Sam pushed him towards his roan until his chest touched the horse, then grabbed him by the ankles and heaved him over the saddle. He would have a thumping head on him by the time they reached Wilton, dangling from the waistline, his legs the other side, but that might make him more amenable to questioning. Right now he'll tell me nothing, Buck decided, not even his name.

He moved to his right to look at the recumbent man a few yards away. There was a blood-stain on his shirt where the rifle bullet had thumped into his heart and Sam Buck knew there was nothing he could do for the unfortunate murder victim. He went through his pockets, looking for something that might tell him who the man was and why he had become the target for assassination, apart from the elementary reason of robbery.

He found a letter addressed to Mr Gene Farrow at the Post Office in Goldwell. He pulled the single sheet of paper from its envelope and read the message. Gene Farrow hailed from a ranch in New Mexico and although the message did not explicitly say so, Buck surmised he had been on a buying mission into Texas. He returned the letter to the man's pocket, then collected the moneybelt, bulging with greenbacks, and pushed it into his own saddlebag. Then he collected the sniper's gunbelt with its lethal Smith and Wesson revolver and hung it around the sorrel's saddle horn, before returning to the killer's roan. He led him to join his own sorrel and climbed aboard, then set the two horses to rejoin Melissa Nevin, wondering if the man he had taken into custody selected his victims from specific knowledge or whether he simply took pot luck as to what they might be carrying. Already he was wondering if he had stumbled upon the very man Sheriff Emerson was looking for, in spite of the more southern area the sniper had selected for this particular strike.

She was moving her pony slowly towards him as Buck and his prisoner reached the bend in the trail. Buck turned both horses and waited for her to rejoin him.

'What happened, Sam?'

He nodded towards the unknown man draped uncomfortably across the saddle of the horse he was leading. 'This scumbag rifle-shot a man lying just off the trail up ahead. I'll hand him over to the marshal in Wilton. I want you to take charge of the dead man. I'll put him on his own horse when we get back there.'

She stared back at him uneasily, her senses

affronted by the very fact of death. The loss of her own mother and the memory of having to see her lifeless in her burying box was still etched deeply on her mind. Death was something abhorrent to her, but she knew they could not leave this unfortunate victim of a sniper's bullet to the mercy of the scavengers. She took a deep breath and accepted what had to be done. 'All right, Sam.'

After an hour, his head bursting with too much blood circulating around his skull, the prisoner arched himself and slid from his horse. Buck halted and climbed down to look at him with more than disgust.

'Head bothering you, is it? I thought it might.'

'Why can't you let me sit in the saddle like any normal human bein'?'

'Because you ain't a normal human being. You're a lowdown skunk who kills men from ambush.'

'If you think I'm gonna ride any further

bellied over that saddle you'll have to tie me down.'

'That can easily be arranged. On the other hand, give me some cooperation and I'll let you sit that saddle.'

The man ignored the offer and went on complaining. 'My arms and shoulders are killin' me. Take this belt off o' me!'

Sam Buck hinged his knees and bent over him. 'You got a name?'

The beady blue eyes looked back at the Ranger, wondering what he might gain by the cooperation he'd been invited to offer. He decided to try out his captor's promise. 'Headley. Mike Headley,' he conceded.

'And how many other men have you shot from ambush, Headley?'

The blue eyes narrowed and Headley's voice was defiant. 'I'm not keepin' score.'

'I'd reckon at least four north of Goldwell, for starters.'

Melissa Nevin had sat her pony silently while the exchanges had been taking place, but now she spoke up sharply. 'You think he killed my uncle, Sam?'

'I'd say it's more than likely, Melissa.'

'You murdering swine!' she spat at Headley. 'If I'd gotten a gun I'd kill you myself and save the hangman a job.'

Sam Buck was surprised by the ferocity of the girl's anger. He stared at her for a full half minute before deciding to take a look in Headley's saddlebags. They were bulging with currency notes and a fair sample of silver dollars.

'Seems to me you owe this young lady two thousand dollars, Headley. Can I give it back to her now? You took it off Boris Dillinger after you'd killed him.'

'Who told you that?'

'Marshal Brundle, back in Goldwell.'

Headley looked up at Melissa. 'You Dillinger's daughter?'

'He didn't have a daughter. I'm his niece, his nearest relative, so that money belongs to me.'

Hoping to curry more favour, Headley looked at Buck and said, 'Give it to her if it'll make you happy.'

Buck's tone was heavy with sarcasm. 'You sure you want me to do that?'

'Give it to her!'

'So you admit killing Boris Dillinger?'

'Yes! Yes! Get this damn belt off of my arms.'

'Any more killings you want to confess to?'

They could only hang him once, Headley reasoned, so there was no need to be modest about his successes. 'You mean those other three north of Goldwell?'

Buck nodded. 'And any more you care to accept responsibility for killing.'

A sly smile. 'Sure, I killed more. I'm good, as you might have noticed.'

'How about rancher Chuck Felton?'

'Naw. Cain't oblige you with that one.'

'Jack Kerrigan?'

Pride in his marksmanship prevented him from denying any other killings and he smiled with malice. 'Could be. I don't keep a record o' names.'

'I guess we have gotten enough evidence

to hang you.'

'So how about my arms?'

Buck went to his own saddlebags and fished for a pair of manacles. 'We'll use these instead of the belt.'

Headley's arms and shoulders were locked in stiffness and before he could flex them Sam Buck had his wrists manacled, but this time in front of his body. 'You can ride saddle now, but don't get any ideas. I'm entitled to shoot a prisoner trying to escape, and don't you forget it.'

'You reckon you could stretch your generosity to fixin' that belt around my pants again?'

Buck stood behind Headley and handed the belt end and the buckle to him. 'Can you manage to buckle it yourself?' he said with irony.

Then Buck pulled Headley's rifle from its pouch and shucked out the spare shells remaining in the magazine, then replaced it. He raked Headley with a meaningful stare. 'A rifle without shells is about as useless as a man without teeth staring at a plate of beef steak.'

Buck hauled out the money from Headley's saddlebags, counted out two thousand dollars and handed them to Melissa. She shoved the greenbacks inside her shirt, while Buck transferred the remainder of the stolen money to his own saddlebags. He would bank it when he returned to Goldwell.

As an afterthought struck him he rifled through Headley's pockets and found more money. Then he felt around the man's midriff and discovered a moneybelt. When Headley began protesting vigorously, Buck threw him to the ground and soon got the better of him. He removed the belt and counted the contents.

He looked at the killer. 'Another thousand dollars. You were well on the way to becoming a rich man, Mike Headley.'

'You put that back! It's mine!'

Buck's eyes narrowed. 'The question is, who did it belong to before it came into your possession?'

Without waiting for an answer, Buck put the money back into the belt, together with what had been in Headley's pockets, and added the loot to what he had already transferred to his own saddlebags. The bulge was noticeable.

Seething with rage, Headley worked his arms and shoulders until they were loose enough for him to be able to haul himself aboard his horse. His position, he admitted to himself, was the worst he had ever been in, but he still cherished hopes of making a break at some stage before they got into Wilton, and Sam Buck knew it.

'You lead the way, Headley. I'll be right behind you.'

It was dark before they reached Wilton and pulled up outside the law office. Marshal Avery was well acquainted with Melissa Nevin and showed his surprise at seeing her again so soon when she obeyed Sam Buck's instruction to go into the office and acquaint the lawman of the situation.

'There's a dead man outside, Marshal.'

'Is that a fact.'

He rose from his chair and headed for the door. Looking into the eyes of Sam Buck and then at the gun in his hand trained on Mike Headley, the questions began to prowl through his think-box. Melissa Nevin came to stand beside him.

'I thought we'd seen the last of you, Melissa.'

A much smaller man than the law officer in Goldwell, Avery looked at the corpse, draped over his horse, and said, 'Who is he?'

'You don't know him?' Buck asked.

'Stranger to me.'

Melissa said, 'He killed my Uncle Boris, Marshal. He admitted it, didn't he, Sam?'

'He did. Suppose we get this killer into one of your cells, Marshal, then we can talk some,' Buck suggested.

The marshal looked from him to Melissa and then back again. 'You an' Melissa...?'

'We can talk about that, too.'

Marshal Avery was more than willing to lock up the prisoner while Sam Buck showed him his credentials and related what had happened.

'The man we brought in has admitted responsibility for more murders around the Goldwell area, Marshal. I reckon he figures we can only hang him once, no matter how many men he's killed. I'd like you to hold him until I can arrange for him to be taken back to Goldwell to stand trial.'

The marshal nodded, then turned to Melissa Nevin again. 'You heard the prisoner make those admissions, Melissa?'

'I did, Marshal Avery.'

'You'd be prepared to give evidence in court to that effect?'

'I'd be delighted!'

The curl of her lips told him there was hate in her heart and he guessed the murder of her uncle had hit her hard. Then she lowered her head as her eyes filled with tears. Sam Buck came to her rescue. 'Why don't you go and book us a couple of rooms at the hotel, Melissa?'

She sniffed, stood up, and said, 'All right, Sam.'

When the door closed behind her the marshal said, 'You two got somethin' goin', Mr Buck?'

Buck leaned forward, ignoring the question. 'Did nobody in this town try to stop her riding that trail alone? She's an innocent in an ugly world!'

EIGHT

He slept well that night, having developed the gift of being able to switch off from the day's events. In the morning he breakfasted with Melissa Nevin, who seemed remarkably preoccupied and hardly said a word, while Buck considered how best to break the news that he did not want her to go on with him to Houston.

'What's troubling you, Melissa?'

She shifted sad eyes to meet his, then lowered them again, and he guessed she was having trouble putting her thoughts into words. Eventually she said, 'Being back here reminds me of my mother, and now my uncle is dead. What am I going to do?'

He suspected she was hoping he would take responsibility for her, but that was something he could not do. She was a town girl, while he was a hunter of killers, always on the move. Compassion was not lacking in Sam Buck's make-up, but sympathy for the girl's plight could not be allowed to over-ride practicality.

'You must have made friends here, Melissa. I think you should stay a while and see if one of them will take you in for a spell, until you've had more time to deal with your grief.'

'You mean you don't want me with you? You said I could go with you to Houston.'

'That was before we captured that killer, and my ride to Houston is not a social thing. I'm on the trail of an escaped convict. I don't expect you to understand what that entails, Melissa, but if I succeed in tracking him down, it could get ugly. You could get in the way of me doing my job.'

'But you said you'd be going back to Goldwell.'

'So I will, but you don't know anyone in Goldwell, so I can't see what you'd gain by going there.'

'I need to get away from Wilton; make a new start somewhere.'

Buck could understand her feelings, but she was obviously not giving much thought to the difficulties. 'It's easier to make a new start amongst people you know, Melissa.'

The look she fixed on him said she didn't agree.

'I'll be back here in a few days, so why don't you take the time to consider what I've said, then we can talk some more when I get back.'

'You really mean that? You'll be back?'

'I promise. While I'm gone, put that money you got from Headley in the bank for safe keeping.'

Hopefully he would have a prisoner to escort back to Waco. It was a hell of a long way from Houston and he was hoping some alternative jail could be arranged for Dick Conroy to serve his sentence, but if he found him in Houston he would try and work that out with the authorities there. Men like Conroy did not stay in one place for too long and it was conceivable he would have moved on by the time Buck reached Houston.

Melissa Nevin reluctantly accepted she had little alternative but to agree, with nothing to gain by rejecting Buck's advice. He drained his coffee cup and stood up.

'The sooner I get started the sooner I'll be back. Don't you sit around and mope, Melissa. Look up your friends, like I said.'

'Yes, all right.'

He flashed her an encouraging smile. 'You take care now.'

She watched him walk away with an ache in her heart she had never experienced before. The loss of her mother had been very painful, but this was a different kind of pain, and she recognised that for the first time in her life she had fallen in love. She didn't understand it and she certainly did not like it.

Houston was arguably the most thriving of all Texas communities at that stage in the history of the State, yet Sam Buck never likened his mission to the proverbial 'looking for a needle in a haystack'. He was well acquainted with the kind of places to which Dick Conroy would gravitate, and within twelve hours he found him. His badge now on display for all to see, he watched Conroy climb the stairs in a seedy tavern-cum-bordello, his arm around a black-eyed whore. He followed at a discreet distance, noted the room the couple entered, then waited on the landing to give Conroy time to divest himself of his clothing.

'You looking for someone special, mister?' another of the prostitutes inquired as she emerged from the room to his right. A smile was fixed on her freshly painted face.

He flashed his teeth and nodded. 'I am, but thanks for asking.'

Her face registered disappointment, but then she headed down the stairs in search of another sucker.

Buck drew his gun from the holster,

turned the door knob slowly and quietly with his left hand, discovered it had not been locked, threw open the door and leapt inside, just as Conroy was spreading himself across the willing woman. The fugitive rolled off her as she screamed in protest, 'Get outa here, you big lug! Wait your turn!'

Buck smiled broadly. 'You should've locked the door, lady.'

It was only then that she noticed the gun in his right hand. He closed the door and leaned against it. As he had expected, the key had been removed from the lock, mainly for the women's protection in case her client became violent. He watched Conroy's passion die as the little man looked at the gun pointing at his belly and then noted the badge on Buck's vest.

'A bloody lawman!' he spat with a sneer.

'Get dressed, you're coming with me. You, lady, cover yourself up before you catch a chill.'

Conroy reached for his pants and began to pull them on. Buck moved towards the chair standing beside Conroy, where he had dropped his gunbelt, intent on relieving the killer of any temptation. He reckoned without the fast reflexes of the younger man, whose left arm swung swiftly and venomously, catching Buck in the mouth and making him stagger backwards, losing his balance and toppling to the floor near the door. When he focussed his eyes again the fugitive had a gun in his hand and was already in the act of aiming it at the Ranger. They both fired at the same time, but Buck's aim was the more accurate.

He felt a burning pain as Conroy's slug creased his upper left arm, but had the satisfaction of seeing the young killer bend at the waist from the shock of a bullet tearing into his belly. A second squeeze on the trigger sent another leaden slug straight into Conroy's heart. He crumpled untidily beside the bed as the woman screamed her head off in a fit of terror.

Buck bolstered his gun and pushed a hand into his pocket to find a handkerchief to wipe away the blood from his mouth.

He remained in Houston just long enough to make inquiries about the men Mike Headley had confessed to killing, and to see Dick Conroy's body consigned to the grave, then set off back to Wilton, arriving soon after noon the following day.

Melissa Nevin did not greet him with the smile of welcome he had confidently expected. Her face was grave and he knew something had gone badly awry.

'You don't seem glad to see me, Melissa.'

She blurted out the words she knew would explain what was troubling her. 'Mike Headley escaped last night.'

NINE

'Escaped!' The anger that rapidly built up inside the Ranger was plain for the girl to see as his face hardened. It was what she had feared.

'How?'

'I'm not really sure. I've only heard rumours. You'd best ask Marshal Avery.'

He strode from the hotel, marched down the street, and stormed into Avery's office. The marshal eyed him cautiously but Buck was too furious to notice. 'What happened, Marshal?'

'He suckered my deputy while I was asleep.'

'How?'

'Quinn says he don't remember. He was still unconscious when I found him lyin' on the floor this mornin'.'

'Well what the hell are you doing sitting here? Why haven't you gone after Headley?'

'Not my job, Mr Buck. I'm town marshal here in Wilton, not the county sheriff.' His attitude angered Buck. 'Besides, he'd gotten several hours start. Would have been a waste o' time.'

It was no more than Buck had expected to hear, but he had to vent his spleen on somebody and Avery was the only man handy. 'Is that all you can say? No apology? No "Sorry, Mr Buck, I guess we let you down?" No concern that a mass killer escaped from your custody, free to go and kill again?'

'You have my apology.'

'Thanks for nothing! Now I've got to go and chase after Headley without even knowing which direction he took!'

'I guess that about sums it up. He could've gone north, south, east or west. It's tough luck.'

Buck felt like smashing the marshal's teeth down his throat, but he had sense enough, in spite of his fury, to know it would help no one, especially Headley's next victim. He turned and went out into the street again, slamming the door forcibly.

He stood for a moment, then walked back to the hotel, mindful that Headley had no money and would be looking to get some in the only way he seemed to favour. He might have robbed the deputy of any money he had in his pockets, but that was unlikely to last Headley for long. It was a reasonable assumption that the man had armed himself, probably with his own rifle, before he had departed from Avery's office. He considered going back to ask the marshal, but he figured there was no need. Headley would not have left Wilton without the means to ambush some poor innocent and rob him of what he was carrying. What irritated Buck more than anything was not knowing in which direction to start looking. The sense of helplessness took its grip on him.

He entered the hotel and found Melissa Nevin standing in the lobby. 'Hello, Melissa.'

'Did you find out?'

'Nothing of any use. Headley could be anywhere, twenty miles in any direction. He could have me running around in circles trying to find him.' He sighed heavily. 'I guess I'd best get back to Goldwell and bank that money Headley got with his killing and robbing.'

She looked so forlorn and vulnerable as she pleaded, 'You'll take me with you?'

He pasted a smile on his face and said, 'Why don't we talk some over a cup of coffee? My throat feels like a rasp.'

She guided him to the diner down the street and they found an unoccupied table with no difficulty.

He looked around and said, 'This the place where you worked?'

'Yes. I came here yesterday, trying to ease the pain of my memories, but it's no use, Sam. I want to get away.'

She was greeted warmly by the middle-aged woman who came to collect their order and Melissa asked for two cups of coffee.

'You're not hungry, Melissa?' Buck asked.

'I suppose I could eat something.'

'Good. It seems a long time since I ate.' He looked at the woman standing waiting. 'Anything will do. Surprise me.'

'Yes, sir.' She looked at the girl. 'I know what you like, Melissa.'

When the woman departed Buck got down to some serious discussion. 'Did you put that money in the bank, like I told you?'

'Yes, but I'll need to get it out again if I'm coming to Goldwell with you.'

His hopes plummeted. 'Is that what you really want?'

'Yes. A new start, away from all the memories.'

'I could take you with me, Melissa, but once we get there, it'll be up to you to make your own way. I'll be too busy to help you, working with the county sheriff.'

She smothered her disappointment, accepting that a man had his duties and, despite her feelings for him, she recognised that Sam Buck had only ever offered her kindness and consideration. She had no right to expect anything more. It was some comfort to know that she could spend the next couple of days with him. Once they got to Goldwell she would deal with the pain of parting.

They ate in companionable silence, she returning his smiles that offered no more than friendship.

'At least I can confirm whatever you have to tell the county sheriff about that horrible Headley man, Sam.'

'I'd appreciate that, Melissa, though I don't reckon he'd doubt my word.'

'Nice to have it confirmed though, huh?'

They made an early start the next day. Shivers of apprehension caressed his back more than once as Sam Buck tried to recall how much they had talked in Headley's presence on the first ride into Wilton. Did the killer know Buck would be returning to Goldwell with all that money and was he lying in wait, ready to send a lethal bullet thudding into his back or chest once they came within range? And when he saw that Melissa Nevin was with him, would he shoot her too? He would suspect the girl had spent some of that two thousand dollars, but he would also guess the bulk of it was still in her possession. Did Headley have any aversion to killing young women? Would he simply wound her and then gratify himself with her before silencing her for good?

He shook himself to disperse his gloomy thoughts. There was simply no answer to the questions that plagued him, yet he knew that Headley was a master of the art of ambush. If the killer was intent on retrieving what Buck had taken from him, then the Ranger was never likely to find out. He would be dead meat before Headley descended on the young woman. Thankfully his fears had apparently not occurred to Melissa. Each time he glanced her way she gave him a shy smile. He was not slow to recognize she had a crush on him. Better for her to think that way until they arrived in Goldwell, rather than entertain the possibility they might never make it.

The bellowing of a bull, the bawling of cows and steers, drowned the more plaintive notes of newly-born calves as they rode through cattle country. A big oak offered a mushroom of shade as the sun reached its hottest and they rested for an hour, boiling coffee and chewing on the bread and meat they had provided for the journey.

Farther on, towards nightfall, they encountered brush of chapparal, mesquite, and catclaw. Silence enveloped them as the sun sank and, on the distant horizon, turned the sky into a flood of crimson. Away to their left Buck spotted a log dwelling place and decided to find out if they could get a bed for Melissa, rather than have her sleep beside him under the stars. As they drew nearer smoke poured lazily from a tin chimney.

Sam Buck heaved a sigh of relief for having got this far without any of his fears coming to fruition. The thought occurred to him that maybe Mike Headley did not have the brains to realize most of the money that had been taken from him was there for the taking before Buck got back to Goldwell, only the Ranger did not believe it. The man was as cunning as a snake.

A black-bearded man emerged from the house, a rifle held steadily in his hands, aimed at Buck, as they approached.

'No need for the rifle, friend. We intend you no harm.'

'I reckon you want somethin', or you wouldn't be here.'

'Wondered if you might cope with two guests for supper, and maybe have a spare bed for the young lady.'

The biggest man Buck had ever seen hesitated. 'You got money?'

'We can pay you for your trouble, mister, but what happened to southern hospitality?'

'I reckon they left it in Louisiana. A man has to make a dollar any way he can these days.'

Melissa spoke up. 'Let's move on, Sam. We don't want to stay where we're not welcome.'

A tooth-gapped grin showed through the bushy growth of hair around the man's mouth. 'Now don't be hasty, young woman. I never said you weren't welcome. Long as you can pay, step right down.'

He lowered the rifle as his gesture of goodwill.

Buck said, 'We wouldn't want to put you out none.'

'There's coffee on the stove an' beef stew warmin'. My teeth don't chew steaks so easy no more.'

'Where's your wife?' Melissa inquired suspiciously.

'Don't have no wife, missy.' Narrowed eyes looked from her to Sam and back again. 'You two ain't hitched?'

'No, we're not married,' Sam said evenly.

When they made no move to dismount his irritation showed. 'Well you wanna eat or not?'

'I can smell that stew from here,' Buck said. 'Reckon it could be mighty appetising.'

'Oh, it is. I feed myself good.'

Sam Buck climbed down from his saddle and looked at Melissa with a smile.

'We've been invited to supper, Melissa. Can't disappoint the gentleman now, can we?'

Her fear of this man mountain who stood waiting for her response was plain for Buck to see, but so long as he was there with her, what was there to fear? She eased herself down.

'Best bring your own plates in with you,' their host suggested. 'Reckon you'd feel better with your own things than these old things I've gotten.'

The quality of the stew was surprisingly good and they both ate with relish. Melissa, deciding she had been a bit stand-offish with the man, perhaps unreasonably, was moved to compliment him.

'You're a good cook, mister.'

'Man with no woman has learn t'fend for hisself, missy.'

'I suppose so.'

In an effort to allay the suspicions his greeting with the aimed rifle had aroused, he poured them more coffee. 'Where you headed?' he asked.

'Goldwell,' Sam told him.

'Goldwell! Is Brundle still marshal there?'

'He is.'

'Now there's a man.'

'Sounds like you know the marshal well,' Melissa voiced.

He laughed, but the tone of it made Melissa shudder. 'You could say that. He locked me up once, after I'd looked on the whiskey a mite too much.'

Melissa yawned and put a hand to her mouth. 'Excuse me.'

Buck said, 'Now about that bed for the young lady I spoke of earlier...?'

The coarse laugh came again. 'She wants t'sleep in a bed, mister, she'll have t'share mine.'

TEN

There was a long moment of silence as the man leered at the young woman in what he obviously considered an invitation she could hardly decline. She stared back at him with mounting feelings of disgust and alarm, in spite of the fact that Sam Buck was there to protect her against any advances the bearded brute might make. In his turn Buck was filled with indignation, firstly at the uncouth suggestion, and secondly by the thought that this man could even contemplate that he would allow Melissa to be debased by such an act of intimacy. His anger exploded in sudden movement. As he got to his feet he upended the table onto this stranger whose hospitality he had accepted, more for Melissa's sake than his own. The man fell backwards, pinned to the floor.

Melissa jumped up in fright, alarmed by what might happen when the man regained his feet. She need not have worried. Buck was pressing the edge of the rough table under the man's chin, hard-held on his windpipe. The giant's eyes opened wider as his efforts to push the table away proved fruitless, his kicking feet flailing nothing but air, while Buck voiced his disgust. 'You lowdown snake! I've a mind to put a bullet through your thick skull!'

'Let's go, Sam,' Melissa pleaded plaintively.

'Take our plates and mugs out with you, Melissa, and then get mounted. I'll be out in a minute.'

She stooped and picked up the utensils and went outside.

Buck continued to press on the man's neck until his eyeballs looked as if they might explode, then he relaxed the pressure and allowed the man to cough and splutter. While he fought to regain his breath, Buck grabbed the man's rifle, took a hold of it by the barrel, then smashed the butt over his head. A sense of elation flooded through the Ranger as the bearded giant lapsed into oblivion.

Buck moved to the door, irritated by his failure to find Melissa Nevin shelter for the night, but there was nothing for it but to saddle up again and move on. He did not falter as he went through the door, expecting to find Melissa with the horses, already putting the saddle on her grey pony, but a rude shock awaited him.

She was standing by the little mare, her eyes wide with fright, a rifle barrel pressed hard into her spine.

Mike Headley's ugly face was wreathed in a grin, his teeth showing whitely in the darkness. 'Well, now, if it ain't Mr Buck.'

Sam Buck halted, his fury welling up at his own stupidity. He had allowed his customary vigilance to relax, assuming he and Melissa were safe from the possible threat of this sadistic killer, at least until daylight. It would take only a split second to draw his gun and put a bullet into Headley, but the killer's reflex action could press the trigger even in the throes of death – and take Melissa Nevin with him.

'I'd be obliged, Mr Buck,' the voice mockingly polite, 'if you'd unbuckle that gunbelt and let it fall around your ankles. You know I ain't squeamish when it comes to a little killin'.'

There was no alternative but to obey, and Buck did just that.

'Now step back an' kick the belt an' the gun this way.'

Again Buck complied, but by now the shock of seeing Headley again so un-expectedly was over and his brain was working again.

He smiled. 'And there was me thinking I'd have a job finding you again. You've saved me the trouble, Headley.'

'You've gotten it wrong, ain't you, Ranger? I'm the one who found *you*. Figured on taking back all that money you took from me. You ain't gonna be difficult about that now, are you?'

It had been in Buck's mind to take his saddlebags and Melissa's into the cabin at the time they'd been invited to share supper with the bearded man, but he had decided it would be best to do that after they'd eaten and the sleeping arrangements had been settled. He looked at his saddle lying against a water barrel near the house but he couldn't see his saddlebags. 'Looks like you already helped yourself, Headley.'

'The money was my first priority. Figured I could kill you any time I wanted, then have my fun with the little lady. Ain't many as pretty as her around, Mr Buck, don't you find?'

'You trying to impress me with your taste in women?'

Headley guffawed. 'Most times I ain't that partic'lar, but this one has it all. Nice body *and* a pretty face. I'm gonna enjoy her, after I've finished with you.'

Buck knew he would, even relishing Melissa's terror, unless he could find some way to stop him. At that precise moment, with his gunbelt and its lethal weapon lying at Headley's feet, it looked as if he didn't have a prayer. If he made the slightest movement in an attempt to get at the knife sheathed just above his right buttock, Headley could elect to kill Melissa. Alone, he would have risked Headley firing at him, but the life of this woman he had taken under his protection was too precious to risk in an act of bravado. She must already be hoping for a miracle to free her from the very danger he had warned her about days ago.

'Let the girl go, Headley. You can do what you like with me.'

'No chance. I'm gonna have her when I'm good an' ready. Now what was that ruckus I heard goin' on in there? You an' Jake have a misunderstandin'?'

So Headley had been here before. It looked as if he and the giant were acquainted. 'Jake's taking a nap right now. Reckon it's his bedtime.'

Headley was not amused. 'You slugged him!'

Buck made no response.

'Jake!' Headley yelled, shattering the quiet of night. When nothing happened he called out, 'Damn you, Jake, get yourself out here!'

The urgency of his call was met with a long silence, but it gave Sam Buck no chance to turn the tables on the killer. Headley still held all the aces.

'You musta slugged him good. Did you kill him?'

'Don't think so. Want me to take a look?'

'Funny man. I'll take a look myself, after I've dealt with you, Ranger.'

He shifted his stance, spread his feet, and moved the rifle barrel away from Melissa. As he pointed it at Buck's midriff the Ranger threw himself sideways, his right hand reaching for his knife as Headley squeezed on the trigger. The bullet sped away harmlessly and as he levered another shell into the chamber Buck's blade sunk into his body, just above his belt. Another shot went off as he doubled over and Sam Buck hurled himself forward.

He grabbed at the rifle, missed, and fell forward as he lost his balance, but with Headley's whole attention focussed on the pain around the knife in his gut, Buck was able to scramble to his feet and wrench the rifle away. He slugged Headley in the same way he had silenced Jake, then gulped in lungfuls of air in relief at having saved the situation.

He looked at Melissa and grinned. 'I was scared I'd let you down, girl,' he gasped.

She rushed towards him and threw herself into his embrace as he dropped the rifle. 'Oh, Sam, I thought he was going to kill you.'

'I guess I got lucky.'

'Let's get out of here, Sam, before that awful man in there comes out.'

'He won't move for a while yet, Melissa, but Headley coming on the scene like that changes things.'

'How, Sam, how?'

'We'll have to take him with us.'

Stunned into silence by the suggestion, Melissa stared at him as if she couldn't believe what he was saying. Taking Headley with them would only prolong the nightmare situation.

'Get saddled up, Melissa, while I find my saddlebags and all that money. Looks like he didn't have time to go through yours, but you'd best make sure.'

Eager to get away, she did as he told her. Her hands trembled as she tightened the cinch and the pony protested at being saddled again so soon. Bessy won the argument and Melissa never realized she had not pulled the buckle tight enough.

She picked up her saddlebags and found her money still intact. She glanced at Sam Buck as the Ranger recovered his knife. The blow Buck had dealt Headley was only a glancing one and he regained his senses as the blade was removed, causing blood to spurt profusely. He cried out in agony. Buck knew the man would die, possibly before morning, but there was nothing he could do about it. Headley needed a surgeon and Buck had no idea where to find one.

Buck wiped the blade clean on Headley's shirt. He handcuffed his prisoner and told him to get mounted.

'You bastard, Buck,' Headley croaked, 'you've done for me.'

'Don't count your chickens. You might live long enough for me to get you to a sawbones, so get on your horse. I've no intention of carrying you.'

The instinct for life is the strongest in the makeup of man and Mike Headley clutched at the last thread available to him. It was sheer agony for him to get up and move towards his horse, but Buck gave him no assistance. Turning away, he collected his saddlebags and saddled his sorrel.

'You lead the way, Melissa. Head back to the trail. I'll ride alongside Headley. He might need a little help.'

The night was silent, apart from the

occasional hoot of an owl. They made slow progress and little more than an hour passed by before the killer tumbled from his horse and lay silent.

Melissa Nevin heard the thump as his body hit the ground. She reined her pony as Sam Buck climbed down to look at his prisoner.

'Is he...?' her voice little more than a whisper.

Buck felt for a pulse along Headley's neck. It was very weak. He looked up at Melissa. 'Not yet, but I reckon we'd best make camp here. The horses need rest as much as we do. Headley's passed out.'

She felt too tired even to climb down from her pony, but when she did make the effort her saddle slipped and she fell heavily.

'Aargh!'

Her agonised cry sent waves of alarm running through Sam Buck. He rushed over to her. 'You hurt bad?'

'My arm. I think it's broken,' she whimpered.

'Let me see.'

He put his arms around her waist and lifted her into a sitting position. She cried out in pain again.

'Where does it hurt most?'

She was clutching her wrist. 'Here.'

Hesitantly she allowed him to feel for a break, wincing as he did so. 'Yeah,' he said, 'I think you've fractured your wrist. How did you come to fall off like that?'

'My saddle slipped, I think.'

He stood up and went to the little mare and saw that she was right. Her saddle was lying around the pony's girth down one side.

'You didn't tighten the cinch hard enough,' he told her. 'Now I'd best find a couple of splints and strap up that wrist. It'll be painful until we can get you to a doctor.'

This girl's luck seesaws worse then mine, he mused, as he went in search of timber. She's learning how to ride the hard way.

ELEVEN

He knew she would suffer throughout the night, but all he could do to help her was lay out her tarp and blankets and make her as comfortable as possible. That done, he unfurled Mike Headley's bedroll and wrapped it around him, then unsaddled all three horses and picketed them before settling down for what sleep he could manage. Normally he would have been asleep within minutes but he was worried about Melissa, knowing how little sleep she would get with all the pain a newly broken bone creates. At least she would never make the same mistake again when she saddled her pony. Life could be a hard school for a girl who had led such a sheltered life. Her experiences that night would be indelibly sketched on her mind, not least the expression on the bearded Jake's face as he had conveyed the pleasure she could have given him in his bed.

He doubted if she had ever seen a man clutching at a knife in his belly before, and by morning she would probably have to gaze on the face of another dead man. Headley's chances of surviving the night after all that blood-letting were about as slim as a snow storm in July.

He awoke to the crackle of twigs spitting as flame engulfed them. As he stirred and looked around him Melissa Nevin spoke. 'Sorry, Sam, I didn't mean to wake you. I thought I'd light a fire and make coffee. I'm cold.'

She shivered involuntarily.

'It's the shock of that broken bone, Melissa. The pain will have eased off some by tonight.'

He threw off his blanket and scrambled to his feet. Night was losing the fight against the dawn of a new day and her mention of coffee spawned a need within his belly. He moved off to relieve himself well away from her. When he came back she had sturdier dried wood on the fire and had placed rocks around it to make a base for the skillet. Water was already heating.

'You hungry, Melissa?'

'Not really. I just need hot coffee.'

'I'd best take a look at Headley.'

The face was cold and stiff. It was no surprise.

'He's dead,' he said, as Melissa looked at him with a question in her eyes. 'At least he'll never kill again. We can be thankful for that.'

'Will you bury him here?'

'I don't have a shovel. I'll take him into Goldwell and hand him over to Sheriff Emerson. He'll need a statement from you about how Headley died, Melissa.'

She made no response, her mind full of the fate Headley had set out for her outside Jake's cabin the night before. Neither had she forgotten that it was Headley who had killed her uncle for the money he was carrying. Her usual compassion for the deceased was denied Mike Headley. She was glad he was dead, she had to admit to herself.

Sam Buck's gaze remained steadily on her as he waited for her to make some comment. She looked awful, her face drawn and her eyes dulled by pain and loss of sleep. He watched as she turned away and went to her saddlebags, fishing out the coffee beans.

'You want me to do that, Melissa?'

'No. I need to do something.'

'But your arm...'

'I can manage with the other hand.'

She had the broken wrist supported in the sling he had fashioned for her the night before. Best let her get on with it, he told himself. No sense in letting her think she'd suddenly become an invalid.

Sheriff Emerson was standing beside Brundle outside the marshal's office as they rode into Goldwell. Before Buck had time to dismount Emerson looked at the corpse on the horse Buck was leading and said, 'Who you got there, Mr Buck?'

'The man you've been looking for, Sheriff, only I figure there might be another one.'

'It's not Bert Vernon?'

'No. This one's Mike Headley, but I'll tell you more about him later. Right now we need a doctor for Miss Nevin here. She's gotten a busted wrist and she's in pain.'

'Doc Arden's house is at the end o' the street,' Brundle told him. 'You take Miss Nevin down there an' I'll see t'the corpse.'

'Thanks, Marshal. I'll be back pronto.'

'Miss Nevin will confirm Headley made this confession, Mr Buck?' Sheriff Emerson queried after the Ranger had finished his discourse.

'She will, and be glad to. Boris Dillinger was her uncle. He was Melissa's only living relative after her mother died, as far as the girl knows, that is.'

'This Headley ... you say he denied killing Chuck Felton?'

'Looks like he was right,' Brundle pushed in.

Buck shrugged. 'Got a mite too cocky, though. He didn't figure on me having my knife handy.' There was a brief silence as the two lawmen gazed on Buck. 'You gotten any news about this Vernon feller, Sheriff?'

'Not much. Seems he disappeared right after the shooting of that lawyer feller, but there's no warrant out for him, so it looks like the law in Philadelphia don't connect him with Pardoe.'

'Reckon he's a man who knows how to cover his tracks.'

'At least I know who I'm looking for, Mr Buck.'

'That means you'll not be needing me any more?'

'Two heads are better than one and an extra pair of eyes wouldn't come amiss. Glad to have you aboard if you've a mind.'

Buck nodded acquiescence. 'Might as well

see this thing through to the end, Sheriff.' He got to his feet. 'I'll see you later. I'd best get back to the doc's house. I feel sort of responsible for Melissa until she can get settled here.'

Brundle rose from his chair. 'I'll come with you, Sam. Your best bet'll be Kirsten Quinn, widow woman. She has a spare room an' she'll be glad to look after the girl. I'll take you along an' introduce the pair o' you.'

The name Quinn rang a bell in Buck's memory box.

'Did you say Quinn?'

Brundle laughed. 'That's right. She's sister-in-law to that Wilton deputy you mentioned.'

Buck smiled broadly. 'Small world, Marshal.'

'Gettin' smaller by the day, Sam.'

Sam Buck advised Melissa Nevin to say nothing to Mrs Quinn about her brother-in-law being responsible for the escape from custody of Mike Headley in Wilton. 'You never know, Melissa, this lady could be the key to your future here in Goldwell.'

She looked at him with pleading eyes. 'Will I be seeing you again, Sam?'

He gave her an encouraging smile. 'Sure you will. Looks like I'm gonna be kinda busy with the sheriff for a spell, but I'll look in on you when I get the chance. At least you won't have any money worries for a while. You can take time to plan your future.'

'Thank you, Sam, for everything.'

He strolled back to the hotel thinking it would be wise to stay clear of the girl for a week or more. They had spent too much time together during the last week and she had already become dependent on him. She had to learn to stand on her own two feet and make a new life for herself, without his influence. Pretty though she was, and obviously badly smitten with him, there was no place for her in his future. His heart already belonged to another, older woman, and his job was too demanding for even that alliance to come to fruition.

Another consultation with the county sheriff was his next priority.

They had supper together in the hotel diner.

'You think you'd recognize this Vernon feller if you saw him, Sheriff?'

'Can't be sure about it, Sam, but at least I've gotten a good description. He stands six feet one, brown hair and beard.'

'But no picture or tintype.'

'No.'

'He could be using another name. Have you thought about that?'

'Of course. What worries me most is the likelihood he's quit Texas for good. What reason would he have to stay around?'

'You've no proof he killed Chuck Felton, in fact, or Kerrigan.'

'No proof he killed that lawyer in Phili, either, but the tie-up between the three men leads me to that conclusion, especially as that Headley feller denied shooting

Chuck Felton.'

After a short silence Buck asked, 'Has Mrs Felton been able to throw any more light on the reason for her husband's murder?'

'No. I asked her about Bert Vernon but she'd never heard of him. To be honest with you, Sam, I don't really have enough cause to ask you to stick around. You've done your part in getting Headley to confess to the other killings.'

'A man has to get lucky sometimes.'

The sheriff pushed out a dejected sigh. 'I hate unfinished business.'

Buck knew exactly how he felt. To feel so sure you had identified a killer and not be able to bring him to justice was the cross any lawman hated to carry.

'I guess there's nothing more I can do for you, Sheriff.'

'You'll head back tomorrow?'

'Don't see how I can justify sticking around Goldwell, but I did promise Melissa Nevin I'd look in on her again. Must admit I'm worried about that girl.'

'I'll keep an eye on her for you.'

'Would you let me know how she copes? She seemed that keen to make a fresh start here, even though I urged her to stay where she was known in Wilton.'

'Sure I will. I got the impression she's taken a shine to you, Sam. You figure she might want to chase after you?'

'Hell, I hope not!'

They finished their coffee and rose from their seats simultaneously, heading for the lobby. As they reached it they heard a man asking the hotel owner the way to get to the Felton ranch. Sheriff Emerson stopped suddenly, put a restraining hand on Buck's arm, and stared hard at the stranger.

'I'll ride out there in the morning,' they heard the stranger say. 'It'll be good to see Chuck again.'

The proprietor said, 'I'm sorry, Mr Urmston, but you're too late. Chuck was killed nearly two weeks back.'

'Killed!' The man's face registered astonishment. 'How? Who killed him?'

'We don't know. Sheriff Emerson is tryin' to find out.'

In the silence Sam Buck urged the sheriff towards the stairs and they walked up side by side. They heard the man referred to as Urmston say, 'Poor Irma. I must ride out in the morning and offer her my condolences.'

Up in Sam Buck's room, the door closed, Emerson said, 'That man fits the description of Bert Vernon to a T.'

Buck cottoned to the sheriff's line of thinking. 'You figure he was putting on a show of astonishment? You think Urmston is really Bert Vernon?'

'I figure it's more than a possibility. Right height, and bearded, but if he is, why would he show up here now? If that man is the killer, what's he after?'

'Good question. Reckon I'll stick around till we find out.'

The sheriff thought out loud, 'Does he plan to kill the whole family?'

TWELVE

They breakfasted early and were down at the livery stables, saddling up, soon after seven. Urmston had not put in an appearance when they left the hotel. They made good time to the Felton ranch.

Irma Felton was surprised to see them, concerned by the visit, in spite of the smiles they fastened on their faces. 'What brings you out this way so early?'

The sheriff spoke up. 'Just wanted to warn you to expect a visitor, Mrs Felton. There's a tall, bearded man in town using the name Urmston who claims to know you.'

'Urmston? I know of no one by that name.'

Her three daughters came from the stables, alerted by the sound of riders arriving. She looked at them, frowning. 'Do any of you girls remember a man by the name of Urmston?'

They all shook their heads and said, 'No. Who is he?'

'Claims to be a friend of your father's.'

Emily, the elder of the three girls, queried, 'He's here?'

Sam Buck said, 'He's in town, Miss. He intends to visit with you. We have our reasons for investigating this man. If you don't know him, then that confirms our suspicions. When he arrives, we'd like you all to act normally.' He turned to Irma Felton again. 'If you could conceal us in the house, Mrs Felton, during his visit, preferably where we can overhear your conversation, we'd appreciate it.'

'What do you suspect this man of doing?'

Emerson told her, 'We suspect his motives for coming here.'

'What possible motives could he have?' Emily asked.

'That's what we want to find out, Miss Emily. Might be wise if you girls busy yourselves in the stables while he's here. He might not reveal his reasons if he has to face four members of the female sex. If he's alone with your mother I reckon he'll be more forthcoming.'

'The sheriff is right, girls,' their mother said in support. 'I'll tell you all about it later.'

They didn't cotton to the idea, but there was no question of them disobeying their mother. Their upbringing had made sure of that.

'How long before he gets here, Sheriff?' Charlotte, the second daughter, queried.

'We don't know, Miss Charlotte, but we have reason to believe it will be this morning.'

'Come into the house,' Irma Felton invited. 'I'll make some fresh coffee.'

The minutes ticked away agonisingly slowly. Nerves were on edge long before they sighted a lone rider heading their way around eleven o'clock.

The girls went off to occupy themselves with stable chores, while Sam Buck and Sheriff Emerson concealed themselves in Irma Felton's bedroom, the door left ajar.

They were unable to hear the first words of greeting, but when Irma Felton brought the man into the house the conversation came to them quite clearly, with the woman speaking in a slightly high pitched voice, betraying a trace of nervousness in her tone.

'May I offer you my condolences, Mrs Felton. I only heard last night about you losing Chuck.'

'Thank you, Mr Urmston. I wasn't aware that you were acquainted with my husband.'

'No reason why you should. It was a business arrangement.'

'In what way?'

'I have shares in the ranch, Mrs Felton.'

'Shares in the ranch!' Her exclamation revealed the shock Urmston's claim had given her.

'You'll need proof of that, of course.' He reached inside his coat and said, 'This is a notarized document, signed by your late husband's attorney.'

The hiding lawmen faintly heard a document changing hands, followed moments later by the astonishment in Irma Felton's voice. 'Five thousand dollars! You have a five thousand dollar interest in this ranch?'

'Yes, ma'am. I'm sorry if that comes as a shock to you, but my circumstances have taken a turn for the worse. I need to sell my shares in the ranch.'

Judging by his unkempt hair and beard, the sad eyes, Irma Felton could easily believe it. She recovered sufficiently from her shock to defend her position in the only way she could think of at such short notice.

'And who do you think might be interested in putting up the money?'

'I've been giving that some thought overnight. It occurred to me that you might, ma'am.'

There was a long silence before Urmston spoke again.

'Do you plan to stay here, Mrs Felton?'

'Of course. It is what my husband would want me to do.'

'Then it would obviously be in your interests to obtain full ownership.'

'Until a moment ago I thought I had complete ownership.'

At that point, back in the bedroom, Sheriff Emerson made a decision. He indicated with signs that he wanted Sam Buck to remain, while he slipped outside and re-entered the house by the front door. The bedroom window was already open at the bottom and he quietly slipped through and catfooted around to the front. He knocked loudly. Buck heard Irma Felton respond to the knocking.

'Excuse me a moment, Mr Urmston, while I see who that is.'

Moments later Emerson said in a loud voice, 'Morning, Irma. The girls told me you were in the house. Anne is watering my horse. That girl is growing up fast. I reckon she'll turn out to be the beauty of the three.'

The woman responded to his lead. 'Do

come in, Sheriff.'

Emerson stepped inside, still talking. 'Not that there's anything amiss with Emily or Charlotte, let me hasten to add.'

'Come through. I have a visitor I'd like you to meet.'

Emerson stared at the stranger.

'Mr Urmston, this is our county sheriff.'

Urmston nodded and smiled, seemingly not put out by the presence of the law officer. 'My pleasure, Sheriff.'

'Didn't I see you in the hotel lobby last night?'

'That's quite possible. I came to offer Mrs Felton my condolences. It was only last night that I learned of Chuck's death.'

If that's the truth, then you can't be Bert Vernon, Emerson told himself. 'You're an Easterner, Mr Urmston.'

'I am indeed, Sheriff. Philadelphia is my home town.'

'Big city man, huh?'

'I suppose you could say that.'

Irma Felton interposed, 'Mr Urmston had

another reason for coming to see me, Sheriff. He claims he has a five thousand dollar share in my ranch.'

'It's more than just a claim, ma'am, it's a fact. You still have my certificate in your hand.'

Emerson held out his hand. 'May I see that, ma'am?'

She surrendered it with such alacrity it might have been something lethal.

The sheriff read it through, while the other two stayed silent. He handed it back to the woman and said, 'It looks legal enough.'

Her face was grave. 'As you can imagine, Sheriff, it's come as quite a shock to find out I'm not the sole owner of my own home and the land and cattle.'

She sat down suddenly. 'Please, be seated, gentlemen.'

Emerson looked directly at Urmston. 'Far be it from me to question the authenticity of that certificate, Mr Urmston, but would you take offence if I suggested Irma contact this attorney feller in Philadelphia, just to confirm it? I believe there has been a spate of forgeries back east lately.'

The smile was back in place as Urmston said, 'Ah! I'm afraid that won't be possible, Sheriff. Mr Pardoe was murdered a few months ago.'

'Murdered!' Emerson, feigning shock, allowed the silence to hang. 'How very unfortunate.'

'Indeed. His killer has never been found, I'm sorry to say.'

The sheriff said, 'I guess it's none of my business, Mr Urmston, but it seems to me your arrival here has given Mrs Felton a nasty shock. Maybe...'

'Yes, I can understand that, Sheriff.' He looked back at the woman with those melancholy dark eyes. 'Maybe you'd like a day or two to think about it, ma'am, then we can talk again?'

'Yes, I would. Perhaps we could meet at the lawyer's office in Goldwell, the day after tomorrow? My daughters are going to be very upset when I tell them the news, especially so soon after losing their father.'

'I understand. Day after tomorrow will be fine.'

'You should have no difficulty finding Mr Dorsey's office. He has a sign outside.'

Urmston climbed to his feet again. 'Thank you. I'll see you the day after tomorrow. Goodbye for now.' He nodded to Emerson. 'Sheriff,' then turned on his heels and headed for the door.

The sheriff said, 'You sit there, ma'am, I'll see Mr Urmston out for you.'

Emerson had already noticed that Urmston had not been wearing a gunbelt, but as the man climbed into the saddle again the butt of a rifle stuck out of the pouch. The sheriff would have gambled his last dollar that Emmet Urmston was in fact former U.S. Cavalryman Bert Vernon, expert rifleman.

THIRTEEN

Sheriff Emerson watched the visitor ride away, then turned back into the house, calling out as he rejoined the woman. 'He's gone, Sam. You can come out now.'

Sam Buck eased himself through the open doorway and looked from one to the other. 'You really think that certificate is genuine?'

Emerson met his gaze unflinchingly, but when he turned to fix his eyes on Irma Felton he felt his throat go dry. 'Any more coffee in that pot, ma'am?'

She ignored the question and said, 'You don't think it could have been forged, Sheriff?'

He shrugged. 'It's a possibility, but I hate to raise your hopes. It looked straight enough to me. Pity we can't contact that lawyer feller in Philadelphia to check, but maybe Dorsey can find something wrong with it.'

There was a sudden influx from the kitchen and Emily, Charlotte and Anne Felton came bursting into the room, all of them eager to find out what the stranger had called to see their mother about. She looked at them with saddened eyes.

'Did you know him, Momma?' from Anne.

Emily said bluntly, 'What did he want?'

'Five thousand dollars.'

'Five thousand dollars!' Charlotte exclaimed. 'What for?'

'He has proof that he staked your father for that amount when Daddy bought this place. Now he wants to sell his stake.'

'Do you have that much money, Momma?' Emily asked.

'Just about.'

'Then you'll buy his share?' Anne queried anxiously.

'I may have to, but then we'd have no spare cash to meet our bills. We'd have to sell stock sooner than I intended.'

'What happens if you don't pay up?'

'I don't know, sweetheart, I just don't know.' She glanced at the sheriff. 'Do you think he could sell his interest locally, Sheriff Emerson?'

'He might, ma'am, or he might want a say in the control of the ranch. Might even want to come and live here.'

Irma Felton's face registered alarm. 'He made no such suggestion!'

'Maybe he's keeping that option up his sleeve. If you don't come up with the money he might figure gaining some control in your affairs a viable option. Any man down on his heels would jump at a chance like that to get back on his feet, and this one is no fool.'

'Oh, no!'

That possibility did not find favour with any of the girls, or their mother. Their facial expressions told the two men clearly, without the need of words.

Sam Buck pushed into the silence, 'If

there is anything we can do to help you, ma'am?'

'Thank you, Mr Buck, but no, I don't think there is.' She put on a smile for the benefit of her daughters. 'Well now, let's forget about Mr Urmston for a while and get ourselves something to eat.' Her gaze fastened first on Buck and then on the sheriff. 'You will of course join us before you ride back to town.'

After that early breakfast, neither man was going to pass up the invitation.

'Emily, see what you can do for us, while I entertain our guests.'

The three girls went off to the kitchen, but then gloom settled on the woman and the two men, all of them finding topics for conversation in short supply.

Eventually Sam Buck broke the silence. 'Your husband picked a good spot to settle, Mrs Felton. Some of the best grazing in Texas is just west of the Brazos.'

'I don't think he would take all the credit for that, Mr Buck. He would say most of it belonged to the man who first settled this ranch. My husband simply knew a good investment when he saw it, but then he was always shrewd. That's how he made his money.'

'Some men have the knack, others don't.'

The sheriff could see that talking about her husband was not a subject she would favour at the moment and decided to pursue more practical matters.

'Any luck in finding a foreman to run the ranch for you?'

'Emily thinks we should promote one of the men already on the payroll. She reasons it's better to have someone who knows the ranch, rather than have a stranger come in.'

'And how do you feel about that?'

'I can see the merits and the dis-advantages. Chuck respected Adam, but would the other men work as well under him as they might a newcomer? Familiarity can breed contempt, don't they say?'

'Very true, ma'am.'

She turned to Sam Buck. 'And what would you do in my position, Mr Buck? Promote from within or hire an outsider?'

Sam fashioned a smile. 'Without knowing any of your men, I'd be a fool to advise you. If there is a capable hand on your payroll, I'd be inclined to wait and see if he asks for the job?'

'He has already done that, prompted by Emily, I suspect. He's eager to have a decision, and if I reject him I think he might leave.'

'And would that worry you?'

'It would worry Emily more than me. She rather likes him and I think they've been riding together in the evenings.'

'Not a good time to antagonize your eldest daughter.'

'No, but then is he a fortune hunter, or genuinely fond of Emily and keen to prove he is worthy of her?'

Emerson said, 'That's quite a dilemma you've gotten.'

As soon as the meal was over Sheriff Emerson asked to be excused. 'Time me and Sam were getting back to town, Irma. We've things to do and that old sun keeps on moving around.'

'I'm most grateful to you for coming, Sheriff. And you, Sam. You've been a great comfort to me this morning. It was so good to know help was at hand if I needed it.'

'You're more than welcome, Irma,' Emerson said for both of them.

'We'll try and be in town when you come to see Dorsey. If you need us, just holler.'

Once they were on the trail again, riding at walking pace to give the horses a blow, Sam Buck said, 'What do you really think about Urmston?'

'I think Urmston is an adopted name. I'd stake my last cent on him being Bert Vernon in disguise. The signature on that certificate looks genuine enough, but what puzzles me is how he persuaded that lawyer feller to sign it if Urmston is really Vernon, because the man didn't have the money.'

'Oh, that's simple enough, if he is Vernon in disguise.'

'How do you figure it out?'

'If he is Vernon, he held a gun on Pardoe, then killed him once the ink was dry.'

FOURTEEN

When it came to proving their suspicions they agreed they were up against an adobe wall at least three feet thick. The sheriff doubted if John Dorsey would find anything amiss with Urmston's claims, and if that proved to be the case, Irma Felton would either have to pay up or take the risk of someone who might become difficult buying into her assets.

'She won't like that,' Emerson opined.

'I think we'd best wait and see which way Urmston jumps,' Sam Buck said. 'You could be wrong about him, Sheriff. He might be genuine, though I reckon you're right and Neville Pardoe made out that authorization with a gun at his head.'

'I wonder which way he'd jump if I accused him of being Bert Vernon and

142

killing Chuck Felton?'

'Could be interesting.' When the sheriff made no further comment Buck added, 'And dangerous.'

Emerson smiled slyly. 'I was thinking of having you with me at the time.'

After more discussion they decided to invite Urmston to join them for supper that evening.

'To what do I owe this pleasure, gentlemen?' their guest queried as they sat down together.

'You're a stranger in these parts, Mr Urmston. Wouldn't want you to think we Texans are inhospitable.'

Little but banalities were exchanged as the meal progressed, but eventually Sam Buck tiptoed into more productive discussion.

'You ever meet a man by the name of Vernon, Mr Urmston? Bert Vernon, former U.S. Cavalryman?'

No doubt about it, Urmston's face suffused with colour. Then he looked Buck straight in the eye and said, 'Don't recall anyone by that name, Mr Buck, but then Philadelphia is a lot bigger than Goldwell. A lot more people live there.'

'The reason I ask is because he was connected with Chuck Felton back in his Phili days. Seemed logical that you might have met, you being a stake holder in Felton's ranch.'

'Chuck's business deals were very complicated and widespread, as I understood it. He bought ailing business ventures and either turned them around and then sold them off at a huge profit, or stripped them of their assets if they were competing with his other interests. That's how he became wealthy.'

The sheriff said, 'Then how come he needed five thousand dollars of your money, Urmston?'

Urmston was not fazed by the question. 'He paid a lot of money for that ranch, Sheriff, as you must surely know. I think he needed some spare cash for day to day running expenses, that's why he offered me an interest.'

'Has he been paying you a dividend these last three years?'

'Indeed he has, but my other interests turned sour on me, so now I'm in the unfortunate position of having to try and get my money back.'

Buck asked, 'Have you gotten another buyer in mind, in the event that Irma Felton rejects the chance to buy you out?'

'No, Mr Buck, I haven't. Would you be interested?'

'I would, only I don't have that kind of money.'

'I'm sure the bank would loan you five thousand, with that quality of collateral.'

'The bank might be glad to take the problem off *your* hands, if the need should arise,' Emerson told him.

Urmston smiled, but his eyes were cold. 'Thanks for the suggestion, Sheriff. I hadn't thought of that.'

'I noticed you tote a rifle. You a good shot?'

'Afraid not,' Urmston replied with a touch of discomfort which both lawmen decided was feigned.

Buck grinned. 'I reckon you're kidding us, Urmston. I figure you're an expert rifleman.'

'Oh? What gives you that idea?'

'Because I figure you're that former U.S. Cavalryman I asked about a few minutes ago. You are Bert Vernon in disguise.'

Emmet Urmston was not the only one stunned by the surprise accusation; Sheriff Emerson stared hard at Buck, barely able to believe that the Ranger had opted to alert Urmston of his suspicions. What would he hope to gain at this stage?

'That is ridiculous, Buck!' Urmston protested, rising to his feet and knocking his chair backwards. 'You have not one iota of evidence to suggest such a preposterous subterfuge on my part and you certainly have no hope of proving it. Now if you'll excuse me, I think we have nothing more to say to each other.'

'You fit Vernon's description.'

'And probably so do a thousand other men. Goodnight.'

He stormed out of the diner and headed up the stairs to his room, while Emerson and Buck exchanged glances.

'What made you accuse him all of a sudden, Sam?'

Buck grinned. 'If he really is Bert Vernon he'll give himself away. Be interesting to see what he does now. If we're wrong he'll carry on like any other innocent man, but if we're right he might choose to run.'

The sheriff considered the possibility, but then decided, 'Not while he still has a chance of collecting that five thousand dollars from Irma.'

They took turns to keep watch on him, one of them following at a discreet distance each time Urmston elected to give his horse some exercise. He showed no sign of making a hurried departure from the area and, in spite of Sheriff Emerson's prognosis,

Sam Buck began to wonder if Urmston really was the man he claimed to be and simply a look-a-like of the man they were seeking. If only they could have found someone who really could confirm that Urmston was not Bert Vernon. Buck reasoned that Vernon had been having more than his fair share of luck if he was the killer they were looking for, while allowing that the man tended to make his own luck to a large extent. Vernon had planned his campaign of vengeance with great forethought, but even the best of plans tend to go wrong at some point. If Sam Buck and the county sheriff had reasoned correctly, then Vernon had killed three men without leaving a single trace of evidence to connect him with the crimes. If Urmston was in fact Vernon, his luck had to change sometime, Buck told himself.

It did.

Sheriff Emerson walked into the gunsmith's shop to replenish his stock of shells.

'How's business, Gus?'

'Slow, Sheriff, mighty slow. I'm beginnin' to wonder if folks have put their guns away for good. That's what comes of electin' a town marshal they can rely on t'do all the shootin' that needs t'be done. Men don't even seem t'be havin' fun with target practice no more these days.'

'Be thankful you've gotten a peaceful town to live in, Gus.'

'Oh, I am, Sheriff, don't misunderstand me, but you're only the second customer I've had this week.'

Emerson favoured him with a grin. 'Who was the other one?'

'Old Cavalry buddy o' mine. He's big in real estate these days, he was tellin' me. Travellin' incognito.'

Emerson's ears sent a message to his brain and his heart seemed to miss a beat. He fixed his eyes on the gunsmith and asked, 'Was it by any chance a feller by the name of Vernon? Using the name Emmet Urmston?'

The gunsmith stared hard. 'How'd you guess? You know Bert too?'

'I do now.'

He paid for his shells, picked them up and went out quickly. As he hit the street he noticed Irma Felton and her daughter Emily heading out of town in the buggy. Hurrying towards his horse he stuffed the shells into his saddlebags and quickly mounted, then set off in pursuit of the two women. He caught them a mile out of town. Emily drew rein as he came alongside.

'You chasing after us, Sheriff?' she asked.

'That's a fact.' He gathered his breath before asking her mother, 'Any news you'd like to share, Irma?'

'I decided to buy Mr Urmston's share in my ranch, if that's what you mean?'

'That's what I meant. Has the transaction been completed?'

'Yes. He came to the bank with me. It's all settled.'

'You gave him cash money?'

'The banker did, on my behalf. He signed for it and I have the legal papers relinquishing his interest, witnessed by the banker and Mr Dorsey.'

'Where is Urmston now?'

'Getting ready to go back to Philadelphia, I imagine. Why?'

'You've been duped, ma'am. The man who calls himself Urmston is in fact Bert Vernon. If you'll excuse me, I'd best get on his tail and see if I can get your money back.'

FIFTEEN

Sam Buck was climbing aboard his sorrel to set off in the wake of Emmet Urmston when Sheriff Emerson drew up alongside him.

'It's Vernon all right, Sam. Gus Keen was in the Cavalry with him. He told me no more'n half an hour ago that Vernon had been stocking up on shells.'

Buck grinned back at him. 'So Lady Luck ran out on him after all. Let's ride.'

Vernon had left on the river trail, according to Sam Buck.

'He'll be headin' for the railroad, I reckon,' Emerson surmised. 'We should catch him before he can get to the ferry.'

They rode hard but, in spite of the fact that Vernon had only ten minutes start on them, they failed to find him. At the river they questioned the ferryman, giving him a detailed description of the wanted man, but he claimed he had not seen any man of that age, height or colouring.

'He was riding a dark grey!' Emerson snapped in frustration.

'I ain't seen no man on a dark grey for a week or more.'

'Damnation!' the sheriff exploded. 'He's given us the slip.'

'I guess he figured we'd be on his tail,' Buck said, 'so he set out to fool us. We shouldn't be surprised, Sheriff. Everything we know about him suggests he's a right smart feller.'

The sheriff looked straight into Buck's eyes. 'What do we do now then? Backtrack and see if we can spot where he left the trail?'

'Looks like we don't have any alternative. He could've decided to make for the railroad at Waco.'

They turned their mounts and headed back at walking pace the way they had come, the horses already lathered up and needing a long breather.

'The trouble is, Sam, he could make for the hills where there's plenty of cover. It's no easy matter tracking a man going north.'

'That's a fact. He'd know we wouldn't expect him to head past the Felton spread and I reckon he guessed we'd figure he'd make for the ferry, so he led us on, then turned north before we caught a glimpse of him.'

'On the other hand, he could outsmart us by going south.'

'You think we should split up?'

The sheriff was not happy with the suggestion. Bert Vernon had proved himself a man of exceptional talents, particularly when it came to picking off men with a rifle. He was in no hurry to be the next victim, but if things should turn out that way, at least Sam Buck would still be around to finish the job of bringing this killer to justice if they stayed together.

'Not a good idea, Sam. If we are to pick up his trail, two pairs of eyes are better then one.'

'He could be lying in wait to pick us off, and we know how good he is with that rifle. He'll want to see the both of us dead to give himself the chance to start over with a new name now he's gotten the money for it. He's gotten plenty of States to pick from and with us eliminated he can take all the time he wants.'

Emerson stroked his moustache. 'He might get one of us, Sam, but I'd get him in the end if it was you drew the short straw.'

Buck knew the sheriff was expecting him to respond in like manner. 'I guess that settles it then.'

Three miles back along the river trail there was a narrow and little used track that had been made by animals, deer and goats most likely. They decided to follow it, hoping for the sign of a plated hoof print. It was flanked by oaks and brush and not wide enough for the two men to ride abreast. It led up into the hills, verdant with green pasture in the open spaces, and both of them knew they were sitting targets for a sniper up ahead. They remained vigilant, their eyes focused on what was higher up. Buck knew the man they were chasing was too smart an operator to pick a spot for the kill where the bright sun could glint on his rifle barrel and give away his position. Sam figured the sheriff had come to the same conclusion, so he didn't need to say anything.

The stink of equine urine indicated that a horse had preceded them along the track not long ago, but of Bert Vernon and his dark grey there was no sign.

They came upon another track leading off to the left and halted. Buck said, 'He could have branched off here.'

'Yeah, and he knows we'll be asking ourselves that question. Right now he's holding all the aces.'

'What do we do, Sheriff?'

'You wait here, Sam, while I try this track for a while. If I find no hoof marks I'll be back in fifteen minutes. Keep your eyes peeled. Don't reckon he can see you from here, but he might be watching us at this very minute.'

The sheriff set off, while Buck dismounted and allowed the sorrel to munch the grass between the trees. His gaze swept every tree bole, making sure Vernon was not hiding anywhere near. He was equally aware that the fugitive could be concealed *up* a tree. He thought it unlikely. Vernon would have had to leave his horse some distance away and well concealed, otherwise Buck's gelding would have sniffed him out and whinnied. The sorrel was grazing in blissful ignorance of any other horse in the vicinity.

Sheriff Emerson returned just as Buck's gelding left his calling card on the coarse grass.

'No sign up that way, Sam. I reckon he's gone ahead. That's given him another fifteen minutes to distance himself.'

'He won't ride through the night. He'll stop to eat and drink.'

'We can't count on it. He'd need to pick the right spot to light a fire and feel sure it can't be seen.'

It was a thought Sam Buck was not happy to entertain. He was counting on smelling smoke or seeing flame. The nights could get very cold and a man in the open needed a fire.

They rode on, until the sun turned into a red ball of fire as it sank towards the edge of the distant mountains and a shot rang out in the quiet of fading day.

Sam Buck threw himself to the ground and the sorrel veered away as Sheriff Emerson tumbled out of the saddle. Buck knew without question that he was dead. Bert Vernon was too good a shot to miss. But where the hell was he hiding?

Buck waited until the night closed around him. Emerson had not even twitched, never mind moved. Buck's belly rumbled and he silently cursed Bert Vernon for leaving him in the position of not daring to light a fire.

Something had to be done about Emerson, but Buck carried no shovel and all he could do for him was cover his body with brush. It was a far from satisfying prospect but he took the risk of dragging the dead man off the track and cutting the thin branches nearby to, form a shroud thick enough to shield the body from night predators.

There was little doubt in Buck's mind that Vernon was smart enough to know just what Buck would have done after the sheriff fell dead, and on reflection it seemed likely that the sniper had left his place of concealment within minutes after firing the shot. He would have been intent on putting distance between himself and Sam Buck, aiming to find another spot from which to check his backtrail with the coming of a new day. He would sleep without fear on his mind, knowing he was still the master of the situation. Having disposed of one tracker he would see no impediment to getting rid of the remaining one. Then he would be free to pursue his aim of starting over where no one knew him.

Emerson's appaloosa had rejoined Buck's

sorrel and the two were standing quietly side by side. Buck unsaddled and picketed them both and elected to get what sleep he could before the cold crept into his bones. There was cold meat and biscuits in his saddlebags but he contented himself with a swig of water from his bottle before resting his head on his saddle and closing his eyes.

He was up and swinging his arms to get the blood circulating better before the coming of dawn. In spite of having had no food since breakfast the previous day, he did not feel hungry and decided to save his rations in case he was in for a long chase.

He saddled both horses, mounted the appaloosa and led his own sorrel. Vernon was likely to eat before moving on. Getting closer to him was Buck's best way of minimising the killer's advantage. Somehow he had to out-think Vernon to have any chance of turning the tables. If he allowed Vernon to move farther ahead the killer might decide to shoot the horse from under him, leaving him afoot, but with his own gelding alongside, there was still a chance he could survive. His biggest fear was a bullet in the belly, leaving him too badly wounded to get back to civilization, alone and helpless. He had already learned a healthy respect for the devious mind of a ruthless murderer.

Drifting layers of mist filled the hollows as dawn turned into full daylight and it dispersed under the warm sun. The smell of frying bacon wafted his way on the strong breeze that was building steadily. Was it a trap to lure him into a vulnerable position? Surely Vernon was not getting careless already? Only if he felt confident that Buck had elected to return to Goldwell with the sheriff's body would he relax to that extent, the Ranger concluded. Buck didn't think it likely and to assume such a thing would be reckless in the extreme, a risk he was not prepared to take. He dismounted, took his rifle from the pouch, left the horses, and moved forward cautiously on foot, taking care not to snap any twigs and alert Vernon to his position. He was agonizingly aware that Vernon may well already have him in his sights. The smell of food reminded him how long it was since he had eaten, but he could not see the fire on which the skillet had been laid, nor did he glimpse the man he was trailing. He found a hollow near a big oak and settled to wait, counting on Vernon moving towards him.

Buck reasoned that within the next half hour, one of them could be dead.

SIXTEEN

Patience was not Sam Buck's most notable characteristic and he found the waiting tautened his nerves. Lying flat on his belly, rifle held loosely and pointing towards the lower ground from where the smell was still coming, the minutes dragged excruciatingly. As he waited the aroma of cooking slowly dispersed and he came to the conclusion that Vernon was either eating an appetizing breakfast or playing a cat and mouse game. A cold shiver ran up Buck's spine as he thought of the possibility that Vernon already had him in his sights and was simply letting him suffer until he was ready to move in for the kill.

Nothing happened in that first half hour he had feared might be his last. What was Vernon playing at? Did he really believe that killing Sheriff Emerson had released him from any further fear of capture? Surely he must know by now that Sam Buck had not abandoned the chase.

Buck strained his ears, listening for any sound that would betray Vernon's where-abouts. Apart from the twittering of birds he heard nothing at all; no sound of a horse moving off or a human footfall.

After an hour he decided Vernon had foxed him and moved off. Or had he? Was he simply waiting for his pursuer to lose patience and show himself? The need to survive urged caution, but with frustration slowly building into anger, Buck rose to his knees and peered in every direction. He saw nothing but a pair of deer. Mottles on their hides were no more than a trick of the sun filtering through the leaves of trees wafting in the breeze.

'Damn!' Buck exclaimed softly, knowing that deer would not have ventured down-wind into such close proximity if Bert Vernon had still been around.

He scrambled down the slope in the direction he had surmised the smell of frying had emanated earlier. No attempt had been made to conceal the fire. A blackened spot told its tale, the embers having been doused with water. Was it an indication that Vernon wanted Buck to know that he was aware he was being followed? Not many yards away the pile of horse droppings was no more than two hours old.

He went back to where he had left the horses, wondering how much time Vernon had gained while he, Buck, had kept vigil. Maybe Vernon had figured on finding a better spot to lie in wait for the Ranger? Maybe not, but Sam Buck picked on that alternative in preference to any other. Fixing the idea in his mind would help him to maintain his concentration.

Again he rode the appaloosa in preference to his own horse. When they came to fresh water rippling over rocks in a shallow stream he allowed them both to drink their fill, while he refilled his canteen.

The trail petered out in an expanse of open scrubland; just the spot where a man could get himself killed by a sniper who was settled in cover on higher ground beyond. Buck drew rein and considered his options. He came to the conclusion he didn't have any. It could be suicidal to ride across that open stretch and he took the only alternative by riding around it under the cover of trees. The precaution might prove to be groundless but it was better than making himself a sitting target.

By noon he acknowledged that he was lost.

He dismounted and took a swig from his canteen. The pangs of hunger had returned and he reached into his saddlebags to pull out a strip of meat. It was dried and hard but nutritious. To help it down he chewed on a couple of biscuits between bites of the meat to assist the juices in his mouth.

Where was Bert Vernon? By now, he could be as much as five or six miles up ahead, or no more than two hundred yards away, poised to strike. He still held all the aces.

In the shank of the day he came upon a ghost town of old adobe dwellings. Probably three hundred years old, Buck surmised, as he saw the old mission church on the edge of the plaza. The silence was total until a shot whined over his head.

He urged the appaloosa towards a crumbling house, its door lying on the ground to the right of the aperture, the hinges long since rotted. He rode straight through the gap, ducking his head along the appaloosa's neck and dragging the sorrel behind. The horses needed calming and as soon as he slipped from the saddle and grabbed his rifle he spoke to them softly, patting them in turn with his free hand until they settled.

He edged towards the doorway.

A voice called across space. 'Welcome, Mr Buck! What kept you?'

'Is that you, Vernon?' Buck knew it was a

useless question, but he needed more time to place the position of the voice.

'Who else would be here?'

Buck made no response. Vernon was somewhere in the direction of the old church.

'I was afraid you were going to disappoint me, Mr Buck. If you hadn't found this place I'd have wasted so much time waiting for you. Now you're here, best say your prayers. You'll be dead by nightfall.'

The suggestion found no favour with Sam Buck. He did believe there was a God but he was not a praying man. For the moment he was safe. No rifle bullet could penetrate those thick walls. Vernon would have needed a cannon to have any effect.

He yelled across the space, loud enough for the killer to hear him. 'Indulge me, Vernon. Was it you who killed Chuck Felton?'

'Of course. He and his partners robbed me.'

'The law don't hang a man for robbery,

Vernon, so how come you see it as a killing business?'

'They ruined my life, Buck. I'd worked hard to build my business and they left me with nothing.'

'So you killed Jack Kerrigan and Neville Pardoe, as well as Chuck Felton?'

There was no hesitation. 'Right in one.'

'Can I have that in writing?' Buck asked facetiously.

A hollow laugh echoed across the square. 'Be a waste of time. You're going nowhere and the buzzards will pick your bones.'

He could well be right, Buck conceded silently. He knows exactly where I am and he'll have picked the best spot in town to conceal himself. Possibly he has the whole town under his gaze. The thought naturally led Buck to suspect that Vernon was up in the church tower. The Spanish monks who had built the town all those years ago, assisted by peasants or Indians, were masters of the construction business with the materials of their time. That church would be a strong building, stronger than any of the other structures in the town and therefore more resistant to crumbling through the years that had gone.

Buck realized that his best chance of survival was to wait for darkness, but he knew Vernon was not the kind of man who would make idle threats. He had said Buck would be dead by nightfall, so how was he intending to flush him from this old house?

He looked around him. The room was fairly large and a vacant doorway led to the rear. He went through it to investigate and recognised the kitchen area. There was no upper storey and the former occupiers had probably lived and slept in the larger room. He went back in there and again spoke to the horses. To them it would seem a little like a stable building.

Vernon had him cornered. He was trapped. The moment he stepped through that doorway the killer would take aim and fire. The only aspect of the situation in Buck's favour was that Vernon would have to leave his hidey-hole to come and face him if he were to carry out his threat of a killing by nightfall. All Buck could do was wait out the time until he came, then he would have an even chance. In less than an hour, night would engulf the old town.

Time dragged. Waiting, Buck knew, always had this effect. It did not help, but he was thankful the horses had settled. He knew that was largely because of his presence there with them. He also knew that to sacrifice one of them by sending it fast out through the gaping doorway would draw Vernon's fire, yet how would it profit him, Sam Buck?

Vernon's rifle was doubtless trained on that opening, but by the time Buck emerged in the wake of the horse the spurt of flame from Vernon's rifle would have disappeared and he would be no wiser with regard to the sniper's position. The shot sound would echo from within the church tower, if indeed that was where Vernon had concealed himself, yet give only a general direction from which it had come, while he himself would present a target for a second strike. For as long as daylight lasted, Vernon would still hold all the aces.

There was just one chance of escape. If he could hack a hole through the rear wall of the old house and climb through...

He silently cursed. If he even attempted it the sound of his axe hacking away at the adobe would echo through the town. He always carried a small axe with him, so he had the right tool for the job. He cursed himself again. He had been wasting time. The noise would at least concentrate Bert Vernon's attention away from that front opening, even if he did guess what Buck was up to. Vernon would have to try and cover both the back and front of the house and that might not be easy. The thought cheered Sam Buck. If he could actually create a hole big enough to climb through, it would probably be dark by the time he had finished. Not even a former Cavalry crackshot could see well enough in the dark to target a man who could emerge from either of two places. He would have to make a choice; he could just as easily make the wrong one as the right, giving Sam Buck a fifty-fifty chance to turn the tables. He reached for his axe and went through to the back.

'You don't fool me, Sam Buck! I know what you're up to!'

The words echoed across the plaza. Buck ignored them and carried on hacking. He recognized the possibility that Vernon might elect to leave his position and take up a closer hidey-hole where he could still see the front opening to the house, but that would take him several minutes and he would have to cross open space to do it. He would do it by degrees, listening for the sounds Buck was making, and when Sam paused, Vernon would duck out of sight, adding to the time it would take for him to relocate his position. If he should decide to rush the house while Buck was hacking away at the wall, then Sam still had the protection of the intervening inner wall. His axe was falling in a corner well away from the middle opening. Vernon would have to show himself before he could take aim at the man he had waited for so patiently through much of the afternoon.

As his arm began to tire with the exertion, Buck eased himself back to the front of the house with the object of solving one puzzle and also checking if Vernon had moved.

He called out clearly. 'Why didn't you gun me down as I rode into town, Vernon?'

'I wanted to be sure you knew who it was who'd shot you.'

Was it Buck's imagination or had Vernon moved closer to the house?

'No man ever got the better of me, Sam Buck.'

Previously the voice had seemed to come from a position high up, but Buck estimated that Vernon was now down at ground level. He went back to his work at the rear.

SEVENTEEN

He removed his hat and sleeved the sweat from his brow. The dust was clogging up his nostrils and getting to the back of his throat as he gulped for air. The horses were shuffling restlessly on their hooves, disquieted by the noise of banging. He'd been banking on one of them alerting him if Vernon should make a dash into the house, but now their fidgeting had put paid to that hope. He fisted his Colt and eased back to the opening between the rooms.

He stood listening intently for several minutes, while the horses gradually quieted. Then he peered around the wall into the big room. There was no sign of Bert Vernon. He crossed the room to the outer doorway and looked out, without exposing himself. The sun had gone and dusk was ready to give way to night. Darkness would aid any movement Vernon cared to make and would help him as much as Sam Buck. The odds were not yet even. Buck was still trapped and he needed to finish making that escape hole. If only he'd had time to assess what was to the rear of the house before he'd rushed inside he might feel happier about his prospects.

He went back to his task with renewed urgency. It lifted his spirits when he thought of having survived Vernon's threat to kill him before the night came.

The last part of the wall crumbled quicker than he had expected and he lost his balance, ending up on his knees.

It saved his life.

The roar of an exploding rifle just the other side of the hole echoed through the house. Vernon had been waiting for that final breakthrough, confident Sam Buck would be an easy target.

But there was no time to dwell on his good fortune. Buck pushed himself to his feet, grabbed his rifle in his left hand and his Colt in the right and rushed through to the front of the house. He hurled himself out into the night, immediately aware of movement to his left. Bert Vernon was lifting his rifle to take fresh aim. Buck dived sideways and loosed off a shot from the Colt and heard a gasp of pain as the slug found its target, but then Vernon ducked back around the side of the house. The sound of running reached Buck's ears as he scrambled to his feet.

If anything the odds had swung slightly in Buck's favour, but not much. Chasing after Vernon in the dark was fraught with danger. Cavalrymen were trained to spot Indians by night and there was no question in Sam Buck's mind that Bert Vernon's eyesight was as good as any man's, and possibly slightly better than his own. He ran across the street, reaching cover quite safely, then hurried towards the plaza. He felt sure Vernon would head back to the church for sanctuary; not the kind of sanctuary a Holy place was intended to offer a man, but because it was the biggest building in the town and offered options that had not been available to Sam Buck back in that house where he had taken refuge.

The plaza was moderate in size, with the church commanding a noble position over all the other buildings, whatever they may have been. Bert Vernon was probably on the opposite side of the square to Buck, but the Ranger doubted if he had yet had time to get back to the safety of the mission. He strained his eyes to penetrate the gloom, searching for the sign of movement. The absence of it sent a familiar tingle up and down his spine. It was a situation he had been in on several occasions in the past three years.

He catfooted around the plaza in the direction of the church, his eyes probing to his left the whole time. Wherever Vernon had lodged himself he was quieter than a lizard, another trick he must have learned in his Army days. The wound Buck had inflicted on him was obviously not too serious. Painful, no doubt, but hardly life threatening, otherwise he would not have been able to scuttle away so quickly. He could still be on the move, trying to regain his former commanding position over the town. Buck fixed his gaze on the church entrance, hoping Vernon would be losing plenty of blood to weaken him. He was sworn to take a prisoner back for trial in a court of law in preference to exacting summary justice by means of a bullet, but this was one occasion when he pondered his options, if indeed the choice ever presented itself. When it came to a question of his own life or that of the man he had been chasing there was only one answer.

Standing by an old store he paused for a moment to rake the darkness in an attempt to see any sign of movement. Nothing. He moved on just in time to avoid a bullet in his chest. It clipped his sleeve high up as the sound of a single shot echoed across the square. He sent off two shots from the Colt pistol in the direction of the exploding rifle, then ducked into a doorway and shucked out the three empty shells he had already used and replaced them. Vernon had managed to spot him through the gloom and he needed his gun fully loaded in case they came face to face. The man was closer to the church than Sam Buck and Buck did not like that. The one redeeming feature in Vernon regaining his former sanctuary lay in Buck knowing his whereabouts, but he still had to get inside the church himself to get the drop on his quarry.

He ran in a zig-zag fashion towards the church, keeping fairly close to the other buildings around the plaza, then spotted Vernon moving towards the door. He sent two more bullets winging towards the killer but there was no answering cry of pain to intimate either had found its target. Vernon slipped into the doorway and fired back at Buck. The shot sped into the stucco two feet away to Sam Buck's left, suggesting that Vernon was either hampered by his position or he had fired hurriedly, without getting a real sight of his target. His wound must be troubling him, Buck surmised. Otherwise he would not have wasted a single bullet.

Buck crept carefully and softly towards the church, suspecting that Vernon could be waiting for him to show himself in the archway. Second thoughts told him Vernon would treat him with rather more respect than that. Relegating Buck to the status of a reckless fool was hardly in the nature of a man who had planned a campaign of revenge so meticulously; a man whom the Philadelphia police force had never even suspected of killing Neville Pardoe with such ruthlessness.

He listened intently, but whatever Vernon was doing inside the church the walls were too thick for any sound to break through. Vernon would be moving carefully in the darkness. It must be pitch black in there, Buck decided, and asked himself if it was worth the risk of trying to follow Vernon where neither man would be able to see the other. But if he remained outside he might have to wait days for the man to emerge. It was not a viable option. He had no idea how much food and water Vernon had with him, but he knew his own supply was strictly limited. He could grow weak with thirst and hunger just squatting out there, waiting.

Moving to the edge of the doorway arch, he stood listening until his patience snapped. He moved quickly on cat-soft feet through the space where the rotting twin doors leaned drunkenly ajar. His left elbow brushed one door and the noise of impact echoed like thunder, or so it seemed to Buck at that moment. He flung himself full length to the floor as a bullet sped into the timber, the sound of Vernon's shot echoing in the empty building.

Rolling away from the door was difficult with the rifle in his left hand and the Colt pistol in his right and was not accomplished without giving away his position. Another shot thundered through the church and embedded itself in the wall, too high to harm the prone body of Sam Buck. He remained perfectly still for several long moments before attempting to gain balance with the impediment of two guns. Without the rifle he could move much more freely but, although he had some idea of Vernon's position, he was reluctant to leave the long gun where the killer might come upon it.

He now knew that Vernon had not made any attempt to return to the bell tower, where Buck suspected he had taken up position during the afternoon, but the man must know that was the safest place for him to be, giving him the advantage again. If Sam Buck could find the stairway and climb the steps before Vernon made the attempt, then *he* would have the whip hand. The problem was that Vernon knew exactly where those steps were, while Buck could only guess. He climbed to his feet carefully, his rifle held upright by his side so as not to brush the wall with it and alert Vernon to his position again, the Colt held ready for immediate action.

Slowly and silently he moved to the wall, then began making for where he imagined the stairs were located.

Moving one step at a time, then pausing, ate up the minutes which Vernon might be using to his advantage. Buck wondered if the man had a side arm, or maybe a Derringer. At a distance the small hand-gun was not much use, but at close range could be as deadly as a forty-four.

As he continued to listen between each of his own footfalls there was no sound of movement from the other side of the church. Vernon was probably staying put, hoping that Buck would stumble and the noise would give away his position, yet Buck could not rid himself of the suspicion that his enemy would want to climb to the tower again. Once up there it would be difficult to flush him out without the danger of getting killed in the attempt.

Out of the silence Vernon's voice suddenly heightened the tension. 'You're trapped, Buck. I know just where you are, so throw down your guns if you want to live.'

He was bluffing and Sam Buck knew it. Vernon was hoping for some response to his challenge, no doubt speaking from a position of safety behind an inner wall, an advantage Buck did not have. To respond would tell Vernon exactly where he was. Buck used the situation to *his* advantage and moved closer to where he believed the stairs were situated.

'Either give up now or end up dead, Buck.'

At that moment Buck reached a break in the wall he had used to guide him around the darkened church and as he moved another step farther he realized he had come to the foot of the stairway. He also recognized that Vernon was only yards away from him.

'You threatened to kill me before nightfall,' Buck called, then ducked low as Vernon fired his rifle again.

Still keeping low, his eyes now accustomed to the darkness and able to see just a few feet ahead of him, he slipped around the corner of the wall and lifted himself onto the bottom step of the stairs.

'Seems like you still want me dead, Vernon, just like all the others,' Buck said from a position he considered safe for the moment. 'You didn't really think I'd be dumb enough to believe you'd let me go if I surrendered my guns, did you?'

'There was always a chance. After all, once I'm over the Texas border there's nothing you can do.'

'You'll never make it. The odds are in my favour now.'

'You think so? You're forgetting I told you no man has ever bested me. Come daylight I'll kill you. There's no escape from that stairway. You're trapped, Buck.'

So Vernon had deliberately allowed him to make his move, even though he had tried to kill him en route, and Buck accepted the man had suckered him. Vernon was right; the stairway was almost just as much a prison as that old house had been.

EIGHTEEN

Impaled on the horns of a dilemma, Sam Buck stood and considered his options. If he went up to the bell tower he would command an excellent view of the whole town come daylight, but that was several hours hence and would give Bert Vernon the opportunity to slip out of the church under cover of darkness. He would then be able to choose another spot to hide which would give him a clear view of the church entrance, and the chance to pick off Buck as he came out, tired of waiting inside.

Maybe that was what Vernon wanted him to do?

If he remained where he was, on the lower steps of the climb to the bell tower he would be able, hopefully, to track any movements Vernon made. Considering how silently that man could move, there was no guarantee of it.

His third option was to retrace his steps and settle down near the church doorway, giving him a full sight of the interior when the new day came, and wait for Vernon to decide when to make a move. It was not an alternative he particularly fancied. Vernon had missed him three times since he had come into the once sacred place, but a man trained in the art of killing had to get lucky sometime; he couldn't go on missing his target. Buck rejected the idea; Vernon had ears as sharp as an owl.

He positioned himself at the bend in the stairway and squatted on his haunches. It was not a position he could hold for long and when his legs began to ache he straightened them out and sat down, his feet two steps below his butt. Standing his rifle carefully against the wall, he kept his Colt in his hand for fast action.

Dawn was still hours away and his eyelids were getting heavy. He reminded himself his life could depend on him remaining awake and alert, and it was no comfort to know that the same precaution extended to Bert Vernon. It had been a long, exhausting day and Buck longed for sleep. He tried to concentrate on what Sheriff Emerson had expected of him in the circumstances, but that was not enough to sustain his concentration for long. His mind slipped to Irma Felton and the five thousand dollars she had been persuaded to part with in exchange for a forged document that had no value at all. Emerson, he knew, would have done his best to recover that money and return it to its rightful owner, and therefore Sam Buck must do likewise.

His thought processes wandered from one thing to another, starting with a curiosity to know what kind of men were so dedicated to God that they spent all their time building places like this in which to worship and try to convert the Indians who had roamed the area nearly three hundred years ago. He couldn't imagine himself being brainwashed into such activity. Belief in God was one thing, but those men must have been fanatics. He dismissed them from his mind and turned to thoughts of the woman who had impressed him more than any other.

Tracey Ikin was a widow woman he had met in Kerry Town before he'd been promoted to corporal. A few years older than Sam Buck, she had tried to resist his charms, but with only moderate success, Sam knew. He still figured he could persuade her to marry him if he decided to leave the Texas Rangers and settle down. If he survived this confrontation with Bert Vernon he would give it serious thought.

The excitement, the thrill of danger, had become somewhat muted since he'd bid farewell to Tracey and Kerry Town. A man could only survive so many bullets in one lifetime and Buck wondered if he'd used up his chances. A cat might have nine lives – though he doubted that particular precept – but not a man. Most men only had one chance to escape a killer's bullet. Life with Tracey, running a gunsmith's shop some place, had a lot going for it right at that precarious time.

Maybe he'd left it too late? By now Tracey Ikin could have met some other man who put her at the top of his priorities, instead of allowing his way of making a living to rule his thinking.

He pushed the possibility from his mind and concentrated on listening for Bert Vernon moving. Not even a grave could have been more silent.

He awoke with a start, cursing himself for allowing his eyes to close. How long had he been asleep? Long enough to give Vernon the chance to move closer and kill him, he accepted with mounting anger.

What time was it?

Well past midnight, he had no doubt. Maybe even close to dawn.

Where was Vernon? Still hiding behind that inner wall? It must have been a low wall, maybe no more than four or five feet high, considering the man had been able to fire over it and come far too close for comfort. If Buck had only dozed for a few minutes then Vernon had probably not moved, but the Ranger knew only too well that when a man closed his eyes for what he imagined was just a few minutes, it could stretch to an hour or more.

He had to know. He called out, 'You asleep, Vernon?'

There was no answer. Either Vernon had gone or he was not going to give Buck the satisfaction of knowing he was still there. It was some comfort to know his pistol had been resting on his thighs when he awoke, instead of having clattered down the stairs when his hand had loosed its grip, giving Vernon a hint that Buck had succumbed to weariness. With frustration building inside him, Buck began to get edgy.

Dawn came quite suddenly, almost catching Sam Buck on the hop, in spite of his renewed vigilance. There had been no sound in the church and he feared that once again Bert Vernon had suckered him. It really was time he quit being a Texas Ranger and headed back to Kerry Town.

He clasped his rifle quietly and stood up. Slowly he went down the steps until he could see the interior of the church. Light was filtering through the open doors and it seemed to Sam Buck that not even the ghosts of men who might have died there were abroad. The silence was oppressive.

He paused on the bottom step. If Vernon had gone then Buck needed to try and find out where he had secreted himself. He might get a clue with a view from the bell tower. He cat-footed back the way he had come and this time he climbed to the top of the stairway. Looking out across the plaza through the aperture, the first thing he noticed was his sorrel and Sheriff Emerson's appaloosa standing together, away to his right. The crack of a rifle coincided with the ping of a bullet against the church bell. It set the bell ringing, but only for a couple of strikes of the hammer.

He was out there, commanding a full view of the church and Sam Buck's only exit. Once again the advantage was back with Vernon.

Buck squatted as best he could behind the low wall below the aperture that allowed the sound of the bell to ring over the whole town, trying to get a hint of where Vernon was hiding. He was playing the cat and mouse game again, for surely he would have aimed to kill Buck with that shot otherwise.

Had Buck moved just as Vernon fired? he wondered. He had been standing for only a moment in front of the bell, or maybe Bert Vernon was not quite the crackshot he was credited with being. There was the possibility that the wound Buck had inflicted on him the previous night had affected his aim to take into consideration. Maybe he had fired to kill and missed? The thought gave Sam Buck little comfort. Once again he was trapped and Vernon could afford to wait for as long as it took for Buck to exit through that church doorway. There had to be another way out, Buck told himself.

How many years since the Spanish Catholics had left the town? He knew it was no use searching for another, perhaps smaller rear door. Bert Vernon would already have done that, but how old was that bell rope? It looked to be in fairly good condition. If it had been replaced not long before the men of God had departed, maybe he could use it to climb down through the glassless window half way down the stairway?

He took his knife from its sheath but he dared not attempt to cut the rope at the top where it was fixed to the bell; he would expose himself to another shot from the waiting Vernon. He moved towards the rope in a crouch below the tower opening.

Smiling to himself, he pulled on the rope vigorously, the bell ringing loudly and creating more noise than the old town had probably heard in years. Vernon would wonder why Buck was making such a show of defiance, but it would not worry him; he still had the church door in his sights.

Buck allowed the echoes to die away, then held the rope tightly while his knife sawed through it. The rope below his holding hand slipped down to the church floor, and Buck allowed the bell to fall back into its position very, very slowly, counting on Vernon not being able to see the gradual slow movement. He resheathed his knife and quickly descended the stairs.

Collecting the rope from the foot of the bell tower, he hastened back to the stair window, then silently cursed as he looked around for somewhere to fix one end of the rope. There was nothing. No hook, no ring, nothing.

He ran down the stairs again and searched the church for something he could drag up and lodge securely on the stairway. All the old seats had gone, probably used to make fires by the last of the mission town's inhabitants before they left. The only timber he could see were the ancient doors. He could probably wrench one of them from the single remaining hinge that was attached to the framework, but it would be too heavy to drag across the church and up the stairs.

His spirits sank, but the innate resourcefulness of a Texas Ranger to surmount all obstacles came to his aid. To the left of the stairway was a doorway which probably led to the sacristy. He hurried across the space and went inside. An old oak table stood in the centre, probably rejected by the firebuilders as too hard. Hardwood burns only slowly and the old table had no doubt been considered too much trouble to break up and haul away. Buck lifted one end and understood. It was extremely heavy.

He sighed. His axe was back in that crumbling old house and his knife would be useless for the task involved in breaking away a part of the table. But the table was his last hope and, taking a deep breath, he wrapped his arms around two of the legs and heaved, dragging it a couple of feet nearer the doorway.

An hour later, his energy spent and perspiration pouring out of every pore, he sat on a stair and began to gulp in lungfuls of air. The table was heavy enough to sustain his weight on the rope if he tied it securely, but now he no longer had the energy to make his escape attempt. He was hungry and thirsty and, he knew, by now dehydrated. Bert Vernon was settled somewhere with food and drink and what was left of Sam Buck's rations was there for the taking, should he care to chance his arm and search the saddlebags on the sorrel. Buck was almost past caring, wearied to extremes by his herculean efforts. He closed his eyes and dozed.

He had little idea how long he had remained comatose, but once his brain began to tick over again the first question that came to mind was what had Bert Vernon been doing for the past two hours or so? It was essential for Buck to try and locate Vernon's present position before he made any other moves.

He climbed the stairs, leisurely this time, to conserve his energy. Before showing himself in order to elicit some response from Vernon he carefully glanced to where the two horses had been the last time he had been up there. They were gone.

Where?

His gaze raked what little he could see from his position behind an upright. Maybe the horses had grown bored with waiting for him and gone off in search of pasture to chew on.

Or had Bert Vernon collected them and moved out of town?

He crossed the short distance quickly to the other side of the confined space and got his answer. The ping of another bullet rattling the hammer inside the bell brought Buck some satisfaction. He could now attempt to make his way out of the church with the aid of that rope, comforted by the knowledge that Vernon had not departed and left him stranded without a mount, miles from civilization.

It took no more than ten minutes to secure the rope around one leg of the wedged oak table, ease himself through the tight space that allowed light to the stairway, and then carefully slide slowly down to the ground. The rope actually ended six or seven feet from the bottom, but it was no problem to drop the rest of the way and land on the balls of his feet. He lost his balance and toppled over but he was unhurt by the fall.

His throat felt like the inside of a drainpipe that had not been exposed to water for a long time and his tongue was furred up and beginning to swell. His belly rumbled and he broke wind with some relief.

He unstrapped his rifle from his back, held it in both hands ready for action, reasoning that his pistol would not be much use if he spotted Vernon more than thirty yards away.

The handgun felt heavier than usual against his thigh, a sign that his exertions during the morning had weakened him. The sun was now high in the sky and he was glad of his hat, wedged down hard on his head to make sure it stayed on during his descent from the tower.

The situation dictated his strategy. All he could do was search each of the buildings one by one, at the same time keeping an eye out for any sign of Vernon's dark grey gelding. He didn't think the killer would have him picketed too close to his own body, probably hiding him several dwellings away from his own watching post. As luck would have it, he found the horse before he got any inkling of Vernon's whereabouts.

Think, Buck, think. Use the horse to flush out its master.

The animal made no sound as he approached it. He stroked the grey under its chin and blew into its nostrils to establish some kind of rapport. Then he searched the saddlebags, looking for food. No luck.

Vernon had taken it with him and was possibly even now assuaging his hunger. The bottle canteen was gone too, but at least the money Vernon had taken from Irma Felton was there.

Vernon was probably no more than thirty yards away. Buck walked a few yards to distance himself from the horse and sighted his rifle on the mission bell. The ping could have been heard a quarter mile away and would alert Vernon to the fact that he was no longer alone in the ghost town. It did.

He came looking in the direction he had assumed the shot had been fired from and, just for a moment, stared dumbfounded at Sam Buck, his mind unable to accept that the Ranger was no longer trapped inside the mission. Then both men fired at the same time. Unfortunately for Bert Vernon, Buck had seen him first and his rifle was aimed at the man's chest, while Vernon had been obliged to fire from the hip, and that was not his customary stance for aiming. His bullet sped harmlessly past Sam Buck, while

Buck's own slug buried itself in Vernon's chest. The force of the impact sent him stumbling backwards and as his body hit the ground his eyes dimmed.

Sam Buck moved forward and stood over the lifeless body, all threat of danger leaking away. Once again he had survived an attempt to kill him and, with the weakness brought on by lack of food and water, all emotion drained from him. Vernon had threatened that Buck's body would be picked clean by the vultures, but now Buck decided it would be poetic justice to let them have this murderer. He had more pressing problems than to even consider taking the corpse back to Goldwell.

He ate some of the food and drank some of the water Vernon had left in one of the old buildings, then dragged tired legs to the dark grey and climbed into Vernon's saddle. He collected his axe and rode around the town in search of the appaloosa and his own sorrel, but they were gone. Finding them grazing contentedly a half hour later he transferred his weight to the sorrel and held on to the reins of the other two. He must return the way he had come and collect the body of Sheriff Emerson in order for the lawman to be given a Christian burial.

Two days later he drew rein outside Marshal Brundle's office under the gaze of a number of curious citizens, including Brundle himself.

'Emerson?'

It was a needless question, but Buck nodded confirmation.

'Let's go inside, Marshal, and I'll tell you the whole story.'

The following day they rode out to the ranch together to return the five thousand dollars. Irma Felton's eyes were sombre as she watched them dismount.

'Do come into the house, Marshal. And you, Mr Buck.'

Buck handed her the money without a word.

'Are you quite sure I'm entitled to take this back?'

'Yes, ma'am. That piece of paper Vernon handed you is worthless. It was he who killed your husband and his two former business partners. Vernon admitted it when he thought I would never return to talk about it.'

She gazed at him silently for a long time, while he and the marshal allowed the news to settle in her mind. Buck reasoned that it would be some small comfort for her to know who it was who had murdered her husband. He had decided on the return ride to Goldwell that he would not reveal why Vernon had felt the need to kill Chuck Felton. Buck could not shake off a grudging sympathy for the killer, understanding what had created the need for vengeance in his mind. Not all evil men robbed at the point of a gun and Felton and his cronies had mastered the art of what could only be termed legalized larceny. Their actions may not have warranted the death penalty, but there was no way Vernon could have had them arrested and jailed. He had taken the only course open to him. As too often in the past one wrong had spawned another, and history would go on repeating itself, Buck had no doubt.

'Thank you, Mr Buck. I'm most grateful to you.'

He favoured her with a smile. 'Call me Sam.'

The publishers hope that this book has given you enjoyable reading. Large Print Books are especially designed to be as easy to see and hold as possible. If you wish a complete list of our books please ask at your local library or write directly to:

Dales Large Print Books
Magna House, Long Preston,
Skipton, North Yorkshire.
BD23 4ND

This Large Print Book for the partially sighted, who cannot read normal print, is published under the auspices of
THE ULVERSCROFT FOUNDATION